THE
THORNTHWAITE
BETRAYAL

BOOKS BY GARETH P. JONES

The Thornthwaite Inheritance
The Thornthwaite Betrayal

Constable & Toop
The Society of Thirteen
No True Echo
Death or Ice Cream?

THE THORNTHWAITE BETRAYAL

GARETH P. JONES

Piccadilly
PRESS

First published in Great Britain in 2016 by
PICCADILLY PRESS
80–81 Wimpole St, London W1G 9RE
www.piccadillypress.co.uk

A CIP catalogue record for this book is available from the British Library.

ISBN: 978-1-8481-2579-7
also available as an ebook

3

This book is typeset using Atomik ePublisher
Printed and bound by Clays Ltd, St Ives Plc

Piccadilly Press is an imprint of Bonnier Zaffre Ltd,
a Bonnier Publishing company
www.bonnierpublishing.com

Wynne Joyner, 1919–2016
My Nan, who always loved stories

ACT I

A Room with One Wall

Over the centuries, Thornthwaite Manor had survived floods, plagues, civil wars, sieges and explosions. The most recent of these assaults was a fire that had greedily devoured much of the building's innards, but as with the family whose name it bore, the grand old house remained.

The Thornthwaite twins, Lorelli and Ovid, sat at opposing ends of a long blackened table in a dining room with only one wall intact. An ornate chandelier above their heads jangled insistently as a cold breeze blew through the room. A sparsely decorated birthday cake with fourteen candles sat between them.

Ovid shivered. 'We should ask Dragos to take a look at this room next. One wall really isn't enough.'

'I did ask him,' replied Lorelli. 'He said it was not this room's time yet.'

'Yes, that sounds like Dragos,' said Ovid. 'You'd never guess he works for us, would you?'

'Whatever you say about him, you cannot deny that he is a first-rate builder and he is doing a good job with the restoration. The boxing room is almost exactly as it was before the fire.'

Ovid looked uncertainly at the rattling chandelier. 'So long as it's structurally sound, I suppose.'

Ovid's bottle-green eyes met his sister's. A year ago, he would have been nervous that she had tampered with the fitting of the chandelier to make it crash down on his head on the final note of the 'Happy Birthday' song. Or, just as likely, he would have done the same to her. The Thornthwaite twins had spent their childhood trying to kill each other. Attempted murder had become a habit. Now, after a lifetime of murderous plotting, they had called a truce. Their quiet, contained lives of determined destruction had been blown wide open by the previous year's fire. They no longer lived in isolation. Instead of having lessons at home, the twins caught the bus to Shelley Valley Secondary School every day, where they did their best to fit in with the other children.

'Perhaps we should have invited some friends to join us,' said Lorelli, feeling a little intimidated by the size of the cake. 'Felicia was angling for an invite before we broke up for Easter.'

'I'll bet she was,' retorted Ovid. 'She thinks we live in some kind of wonderful fairy-tale castle.' A chunk of plaster fell from the ceiling. Both twins casually brushed the white dust from their jet-black hair.

'We could always ask Millicent Hartwell.' Lorelli winked at her brother.

Ovid's pale complexion reddened. 'Sometimes I miss the old days when we were trying to kill each other.' He picked up a sharp knife to cut two slices of cake, but it was harder than he anticipated and he had to put all of his weight on the handle to get through it. He slid a plate over the table to his sister.

Hazel entered the room. Her light brown hair was tied back and she carried two glasses of lemonade on a silver tray. Since the imprisonment of the twins' cook, Mrs Bagshaw, her adopted daughter Hazel had added kitchen duties to her list of domestic responsibilities. 'I thought you might like something to drink,' she said. 'In case the cake is a little dry.'

'That's very kind of you,' said Lorelli. 'Won't you sit and join us?'

'No, miss. That wouldn't be proper. Oh, and if you please, miss, this arrived for you.' Hazel placed a letter in front of her.

'Thank you. It will be about those books I ordered.' Lorelli snatched it off the table quickly. 'I say, this cake is delicious, Hazel.'

'It's one of Mrs Bagshaw's,' said Hazel. 'One-spoon Cake. Only I added two spoons of sugar, as it's a special occasion.'

'How is Mrs B?' asked Ovid.

'She sounded all right on the phone last night,' said Hazel. 'She's been moved to a low-security prison. She seems happier there. She said she's allowed to spend more time out in the garden.'

'What phone?' said Ovid. 'I didn't know we had a phone.'

'We do now, sir. Dragos insisted we connected one in case of emergencies. It's on the upstairs landing. Will that be all?'

'Yes, thank you,' said Lorelli.

'Happy birthday, miss. Happy birthday, sir.'

5

Once Hazel was out of hearing range, Ovid took a sip of the bitter homemade lemonade and pulled a face. 'I don't know why we don't get a proper cook,' he said.

'Ovid,' scolded Lorelli. 'You know full well that Hazel promised Mrs Bagshaw she would fulfill her duties until her return.'

'Whenever that will be,' said Ovid.

With their parents both deceased, their cook in prison and their head butler, Alfred Crutcher, dead, the role of the twins' guardian had passed to their gardener, Tom Paine, and their former nanny, Eileen Griddle. Both Old Tom and Nurse Griddle exercised a distinctly less hands-on approach than their predecessors.

Tom rarely came into the house, but this being the twins' birthday he stepped over a pile of rubble and entered the room through one of the missing walls. He wiped his grubby hands on his trousers, pulled out two cards and handed them over. Both were handmade using pressed wild flowers.

'Thank you.' Lorelli made hers stand up on the table.

'Why you have to celebrate in this poor excuse of a room I don't know,' said Old Tom. 'There are plenty enough rooms with four walls.'

'It's tradition that we celebrate our birthdays here,' said Ovid.

'If you ask me, young master, traditions are the same as garden plants. You need to decide which ones are worth keeping and which need weeding out.'

'I like this room,' said Lorelli. 'Walls or not.'

'As you say,' said Old Tom. 'I'm just the gardener and I only came to say happy birthday, which I have done, and to tell you that you have a visitor, which I have also now done.'

'A visitor?' said Ovid. 'What visitor?'

'Oh, it's not the Hartwell girl, if that's what's concerning you,' said Tom, making Lorelli giggle. 'It's a fellow by the name of Harry Marshall.'

'Never heard of him,' said Ovid.

'Shall I send him away?'

'What does he want?' asked Lorelli.

A gust of wind caused the chandelier to jangle again. Tom waited until it had settled. 'He's your uncle.'

'Our uncle?' said the twins in unison.

'On your mother's side,' said Old Tom.

'We have an uncle?' said Lorelli.

'Yes. Shall I tell him you're too busy?' said Tom.

'No. Where is this man now?' asked Lorelli.

'He's waiting in the Buxton Room.'

'Thank you, Tom.' Lorelli stood up. 'Come on, Ovid. Let's go and see this apparent uncle.'

The Apparent Uncle

The Buxton Room was named after Lord Buxton Thornthwaite, who in the late seventeenth century had sustained a severe gambling habit. In order to establish whether his visitors were debtors collecting money, he created a spyhole from the neighbouring room, which could only be accessed through a secret passageway.

Lorelli and Ovid found an eyehole each and peered in on the stranger. He had untidy brown hair and a smart linen suit.

'I've never seen him before,' whispered Lorelli.

'I don't trust him,' said Ovid.

'You don't trust anyone,' she replied.

The man stood with his hands behind his back, inspecting a painting of the view from Orwell Hill.

'Come on,' said Lorelli. 'We won't find out what he wants standing here.'

Ovid followed his sister into the other room. He didn't want to say what he was thinking. Even though the twins' mother had died when they were babies and the only picture he had ever seen of her was a portrait that had burnt in the fire, this visitor had the same sky-blue eyes.

'Good afternoon,' said Lorelli. 'I'm afraid we will have to see some identification to verify that you are our uncle.'

The grin that spread across the man's face accentuated his cheekbones. 'Lorelli, Ovid, I can see my sister in you both.'

'Lorelli is right,' said Ovid. 'We'll need proof.'

'So direct. So like Martha.' He picked up a brown suitcase, clicked it open and took out a transparent plastic folder. He handed it to Lorelli. She opened it up and poured the contents onto a table.

The Thornthwaite twins were not predisposed to public displays of emotion, otherwise the room would have been awash with tears as Ovid and Lorelli saw the proof that this man was indeed who he claimed to be. They would have wept at the countless pictures of their mother as a young girl, a teenager and a woman, and at the thought that they were not alone in this world. Lorelli examined the birth certificate up close, hiding her eyes for fear they might reveal her feelings.

'I don't understand,' said Ovid. 'Where have you been all this time?'

'I sent cards every birthday and Christmas.' Uncle Harry pulled a second ziplock folder from his bag, full of envelopes addressed to Thornthwaite Manor. 'You can check the postage dates if you wish.'

'Yes, thank you,' said Ovid. 'We will.'

'They were all returned.'

'Alfred – Mr Crutcher – our former butler, went to great lengths to keep us away from the influences of the outside world,' said Lorelli.

'You could have visited,' said Ovid.

'I . . .' Uncle Harry ran his fingers through his hair. 'I'm ashamed to say that my work–life balance has not been very . . . well . . . balanced. And I feared that since my cards were returned . . . perhaps I was not welcome back.'

'You've been here before?' said Lorelli.

Uncle Harry nodded. 'Yes, I came the day of your parents' wedding.'

'And what brings you here now?' Ovid maintained his frosty air.

'My whole life I have lived to work. When I made my first million, all I cared about was making my second. When I made my second, I set my sights on becoming a billionaire. When I achieved that, I . . . well, you get the idea. I'm thirty-five years old and I have everything money can buy, but I'm lacking one thing money cannot buy. I have no family.'

'You're rich?' said Ovid.

'Yes. Stinking rich . . . Filthy rich. I used to wonder why such negative words are associated with wealth. Why not wonderfully rich? Marvellously rich? It's only when you have money that you learn of all its trappings and you understand. I've been rich and poor and you get judged much more harshly when you have money. Wealth breeds mistrust. Greed does terrible things to people.'

'Yes, it does,' said Lorelli.

'Although money is not entirely without benefits,' said Uncle Harry.

He pulled back the curtain to reveal an expensive-looking jet-black car with a silver stripe over its curved bodywork.

'Very nice,' said Ovid. 'A 1938 Delahaye 165, isn't it?'

'You know your cars,' said Uncle Harry, clearly impressed.

A man with a bowler hat and a small moustache got out of the passenger seat and brushed down his suit.

'Is that your driver?' asked Lorelli.

'No. That's my chef,' said Uncle Harry. 'Beaufort Nouveau. He won International Chef of the Year four years on the trot.'

'Why have you brought a chef?'

'I was hoping to offer you a slap-up birthday feast. I would take you out, but you would have to go quite some way to find a restaurant that could provide a meal to match one of Beaufort's. What do you say? Shall we make this a birthday to remember?'

Ovid looked to his sister but Lorelli was already saying, 'Yes, of course. You are a welcome guest and we would love to dine with you.'

'Excellent,' said Uncle Harry. 'I'll tell Beaufort to begin at once.'

The Chef

Hazel stared at the carp Tom Paine had caught for dinner. She didn't mind cooking for Ovid and Lorelli. She had always looked after them. But she did not enjoy cooking fish. It was the reproachful look in the eyes. Cowell the cat crouched on the shelf above the cooker, watching with equal interest.

'Don't even think about it,' warned Hazel.

She tipped the fish into a pan on the hob and used a spatula to turn it so that it looked the other way. She heard a click and turned to see a man standing behind her. He stood as straight and still as a statue, with his hands behind his back. He wore an angled bowler hat on his head and a neatly trimmed moustache on his upper lip.

'Oh dear. No, no, no . . .' He tutted and shook his head. 'This is no way to cook carp. When frying any fish, one must ensure that the oil is properly hot first – 325 degrees is my preferred temperature.' He spoke at great speed, with a French accent.

'Who are you?' replied Hazel.

'Beaufort Nouveau at your service.'

'What are you doing in my kitchen?'

'*Your* kitchen?' exclaimed Beaufort. '*Non.* This is not your kitchen. A kitchen belongs to the person with the greatest mastery of the art of cooking, and in the present situation, that is I. So, please step aside. I will be cooking this evening's meal.'

He nudged Hazel out of the way and took hold of the pan handle. '*Au revoir, Monsieur Fish.*' He tipped the carp into the bin and turned off the heat.

'You can't do that,' protested Hazel weakly.

'Do what? I am throwing away the rubbish.'

'But it's wasteful.'

'Very well.' Beaufort put his foot down on the bin pedal and extracted the fish with a pair of tongs. He put it onto a plate, which he placed on the floor outside the door. 'There you are, puss, 'elp yourself.' He made a small whistle and Cowell jumped down from the shelf to devour the fish. In a flash, Beaufort slammed the door shut behind her.

'The only animals one should 'ave in a kitchen are the ones you are going to eat.'

'You can't just march in and take over,' said Hazel.

'I can and I must,' said Beaufort.

Hazel met his scrutinising gaze. The smallest of smiles appeared at the corner of his mouth. 'What is your name?'

'Hazel, sir. Hazel Bagshaw.'

'Bagshaw,' he repeated. 'You have lived your life in this house?'

'I have.'

'Whereas I have travelled the globe. I have cooked in the finest restaurants in the world. My art has been appreciated by the rich and the famous. Now, I am here in this . . .' He looked around disdainfully. 'This kitchen . . .'

'Yes, but I have made a promise to take care of the cooking until Mrs Bagshaw returns.'

'Who is this Mrs Bagshaw? Your mother?'

'Yes. Well – yes. My adoptive mother. She's the cook.'

'Is she indeed? And where is this cook now that she would leave a kitchen in the 'ands of one so clearly inexperienced?'

'She's in prison for . . .'

Hazel stumbled over her words. There had been so many revelations the previous year at Thornthwaite Manor that she was unsure how to explain the extremely complex reasons for Mrs Bagshaw's imprisonment. Hazel was grateful when Beaufort said, 'It is of no matter. She is not here. I am. You never know, you may even learn something, although you should know I work fast and I am no teacher.'

'Yes, but—'

'I will allow you to observe and to 'elp me prepare food. I will show you that, with the correct amount of application, one can more than cook in a kitchen. You will learn how to create the impossible.' He picked up a kitchen knife and ran it against a steel sharpener with such speed and precision that a spark flew off. 'Now, one cannot launch a military campaign with blunt swords. Sharpen these knives, 'Azel Bagshaw. And the only two words I want to hear from you are *Oui, chef*. Do you understand?'

Hazel hesitated. This man was overbearing and rude. And yet, there was something in his eyes that made her

14

want to trust him. Hazel had enough experience of deceit to recognise that this man believed every word he spoke.

'So?' said Beaufort. 'I do not 'ave all day. What do you say?'

'*Oui*, chef,' she responded.

The Chandelier

Hazel set three places at the table, then went to the Buxton Room to announce that dinner was ready. Beaufort waited until Lorelli, Ovid and Uncle Harry were seated before bringing in the three plates. The twins stared in astonishment at the dishes. The fish was cooked to crispy perfection and lay on a bed of spinach with almond flakes arranged to look like the white froth of the ocean. Wild mushrooms made the distant snow-topped mountains. The cucumber had been cut into tiny stars, with a tomato as the blood-red moon.

'It looks wonderful, Beaufort,' said Uncle Harry.

'Who cares how dinner *looks*?' said Ovid.

'Cooking is the only complete art form,' said Beaufort. 'Food must appeal to all of our senses. First we consume with our eyes, then with our noses as we breathe in the aromas. The texture of food is vital as it touches our mouths. Then, finally, the taste.'

'That's only four of the senses,' said Ovid churlishly.

'You are right. The sounds are every bit as important. The crunches and crackles we 'ear as we eat is the purest music of all, for it comes from within us.'

16

Ovid scowled at his sister, who was nodding in amazement. 'It's remarkable,' she said. 'It seems a shame to spoil the picture.'

'Yes, a terrible shame.' Ovid dragged his fork across his food and gathered a random selection of food into his mouth. 'It could do with a little salt.' He spoke with his mouth full.

Uncle Harry glanced at the chef, worried about how he would take this.

'Ovid, you're being rude,' scolded Lorelli.

'Not at all,' said Beaufort. 'As with any art form, the consumer is the only true judge. We all have different requirements, and if this young man's tastes desire more salt, then so be it.' He picked up the large salt mill from the side of the room and carried it to Ovid's end of the table.

Ovid held out his hand, but Beaufort kept hold of it. 'Please, allow me.'

'I am quite capable of adding salt to my dinner,' said Ovid.

'Capable, yes,' admitted Beaufort. 'Being capable of kicking a ball does not make one a professional footballer. Being capable of singing in the shower does not qualify one to be an operatic soprano. Capable is not good enough in the search for perfection.'

'I don't strive for perfection in dinner,' said Ovid.

'Ah, but I do, and as author of this meal I cannot allow you to make your own additions.'

'"Author of the meal",' scoffed Ovid. Then he sighed and said, 'Oh, very well, please show how me to add salt in a perfect way.'

'Thank you.' Beaufort turned the salt mill on its side, listening to the movement of the salt crystals as a safe-breaker might listen to the mechanism of a dial. When he had it at precisely the right angle, he gave it a couple of turns, then spun it round so that the salt was whipped up into the air, creating a small cloud. With lightning speed, he slammed the salt mill down and clapped his hands so that the cloud dispersed and the salt came down like fine rain on Ovid's food. The whole thing was done with such precision that only one grain of salt fell outside of the plate. Beaufort took a serviette from his top pocket and removed it. Ovid watched the whole performance open-mouthed.

'Would anyone else care for salt?' asked the chef.

'Not for me,' said Uncle Harry.

'No, thank you,' said Lorelli.

'Then we will take our leave. Come, 'Azel, we must prepare the sweet.'

'*Oui*, chef.' Hazel and Beaufort left the room.

'You take him everywhere with you, do you?' said Ovid.

'Sadly no. He is only with me for a few more days. He is, you see, an *artiste*.' Uncle Harry adopted a ridiculous French accent. '*And an artiste cannot only play to an audience of one. He must spread his wings if 'e is to fly.*'

Lorelli tittered.

Above them, the chandelier tinkled.

'The wind's picking up,' said Uncle Harry.

'I feel no breeze,' said Ovid.

'Nor I,' said Lorelli.

Having grown up in a household more given to murder attempts than most, the Thornthwaite twins were well attuned to imminent danger. They both jumped up from their seats and leapt back as the huge chandelier came crashing down onto the table. They covered their eyes and ducked as several tons of glass shattered.

Once the last shard had settled, the twins looked at Uncle Harry, who had also stepped back to avoid being crushed by the chandelier.

'What on earth . . . ?' he began.

Ovid flung open the door to find a large man with a face as rough and textured as a rocky mountain and a yellow hard hat that kept his long hair out of his eyes.

'Dragos,' said Ovid.

'I heard crash,' he responded. 'You have problem with ceiling fitting, yes? I will take a look.'

The Builder

Dragos Vāduva arrived at Thornthwaite Manor two weeks after the great fire. As with all visitors, Tom Paine had vetted him first and then introduced him to the twins. He informed them that Dragos was a builder from Romania, interested in winning the contract to rebuild the manor.

As soon as he saw the twins, Dragos fell down on his knees and wept. A veritable oak tree of a man, this had been quite a sight.

'I am apologising to you,' said Dragos. 'But this old lady cries out in pain and I weep for her. I must nurse her back to health. You must allow me to do this.'

'What old lady?' asked Ovid.

'He's talking about Thornthwaite Manor,' said Tom.

'Yes,' said Dragos. 'Your home has been badly abused. She can only be repaired with love.'

'Are you really a builder?' asked Ovid.

'A builder?' Dragos stood up and pounded his chest proudly. 'No. I am doctor. I am nurse.'

'We have a nurse,' said Ovid.

'You misunderstand me. I do not work with flesh and blood. I am doctor of brick and mortar. Of concrete and timber. I will return the old lady to her former self. I will only work with materials used in the original construction. She does not need facelift. She is beautiful in her age. This is only way to keep the history in her heart.' He clenched his fist and thumped his heart again.

'Dragos has a good reputation and a low rate,' said Tom. 'Nurse Griddle and I are in favour of employing him.'

'What if we don't want it repaired?' said Lorelli. 'This place has been the cause of so much tragedy over the years, maybe we should put it out of its misery.'

'You should not speak of the old lady in such a disrespectful way,' said Dragos.

'This house is in no fit state to live in,' said Tom quietly.

'Tom is right,' said Ovid. 'We can't live like this.'

'Nurse Griddle and I would like him to begin work immediately,' said Tom.

'So why are you asking us at all if you've already decided?' asked Lorelli.

Dragos replied: 'I will do nothing without your consent. You are rightful heirs. Family must come first.'

'Very well,' said Lorelli.

'Yes, I think it would be good to get the place back to its former glory,' said Ovid.

'One more thing,' said Dragos. 'If I can stay on site I can work with more speed. I have located a suitable room in the south wing.'

Dragos started the next day. He worked long hours and would often begin one task while in the middle of another. A trip to fill his bucket with water would result in a major plumbing job. While he was solving that, he would discover a damp problem and end up knocking down the entire wall. Everything was rebuilt exactly as it had been. His attention to detail was remarkable. Without a single photograph for reference, he was able to restore rooms to their previous selves. When Ovid asked how he knew what things had looked like, Dragos responded: 'The old lady whispers to me. I only have to listen.'

A Surprise
in the Study

Dragos picked up a piece of broken glass from the chandelier and held it up to the light. 'The old lady's teardrops.'

'Teardrops?' Uncle Harry brushed bits of rubble off his shoulders. 'Someone could have been killed.'

Dragos turned to address the twins. 'Who is this?'

'Harry Marshall,' said Uncle Harry. 'I'm their only living relative.'

'How is this possible?' asked Dragos.

'I'm their mother's brother,' said Uncle Harry. 'And you?'

'I am man responsible for nursing the old lady back to health.'

'Dragos is our builder,' said Ovid.

'Your apparent uncle turns up, then this happens. This is not good,' said Dragos.

Uncle Harry squared up to the broad-shouldered builder. 'If I were you, I'd be more concerned about the fact that a poor fitting just cost your employers an irreplaceable nineteenth-century Russian cut-glass chandelier.'

Dragos locked eyes with Uncle Harry. 'It was secure when I checked last week.'

'If you're suggesting I had something to do with this, maybe I should give my lawyers a call,' said Uncle Harry.

'What are you suggesting, Dragos?' asked Ovid.

Dragos shrugged. 'It is difficult to say. I will now check the other fittings in case. Safety must come first. Now you can go elsewhere. Somewhere safe. Perhaps Silas's Study. There is no chandelier there.'

Ovid, Lorelli and Uncle Harry did as they were told and made their way to the study.

'All the rooms have such interesting names,' said Uncle Harry as he followed the twins down the burnt-out corridor.

'Lord Silas was our grandfather.' Lorelli opened the door and flicked the light switch.

As the bulb flickered on, two girls sprang up from behind the old desk and cried, 'Surprise!'

Had either Ovid or Lorelli been holding anything small, sharp and throwable, the girls would have been silenced in a second. Thankfully, neither of them was armed and the girls went unharmed.

'Happy birthday, Lori-chicken!' chirruped Felicia Crick, a pretty girl wearing a yellow party dress with a matching hairband in her straight blonde hair.

'It's Ovid's birthday too,' said Millicent Hartwell, whose hair was a muddier shade of blonde and who wore a plain black skirt and top.

Uncle Harry smiled. 'How lovely. These are your friends, are they?'

24

'Felicia and Millicent go to our school,' said Lorelli.

'I'm delighted to meet you both. I'm the twins' uncle.'

'You're Harry Marshall,' said Felicia. 'You're the thirty-seventh richest man in the country.'

'Just slipped down to thirty-eighth actually,' he said.

Felicia giggled, clapped, then allowed her face to fall into a pretend scowl. 'You never told us you were related to Harry Marshall, Lori-chicken.'

'We didn't know ourselves,' said Lorelli. 'How have you heard of him?'

'Felicia cuts out the rich lists from newspapers and sticks them on her wall.' Millicent's pale grey eyes flickered to Ovid, then fell away again.

'It's just so glamorous!' cried Felicia. 'Now. Presents!' She handed Lorelli a large gift-wrapped box with a purple bow. 'Careful. It's rather precious and delicate. Just like you.'

Lorelli placed the box on the table and removed the wrapping, methodically checking for trigger wires or any suspicious ticking.

'A-hem.' Ovid coughed. Both of the Thornthwaite twins had gone out of their way to hide their childhood of attempted murders from the outside world. Fitting in at school was difficult enough without having others worrying that you were planning on killing them. Lorelli tore off the paper and opened the box. Inside was a glass figure of a girl. Swirling colours filled the statue, but the figurine was totally clear at its centre.

'It's you, Lori-chicken,' squealed Felicia excitedly. 'Mum and Dad made it specially in the workshop.'

'It's wonderful,' said Uncle Harry. 'Did you say your parents made it?'

'Felicia's parents have a glassworks in Little Fledgling,' said Lorelli. 'Thank you, Felicia.'

'I like the way it's got no heart,' said Ovid.

'Actually it has a pure heart,' replied Felicia pointedly. 'Just like Lori-chicken. And don't worry, Millicent has got something for you.'

Millicent held up a small package. Ovid's hand shook as he took it, listened to it and carefully unwrapped the brown paper to find a small white tortoise with green eyes painted on.

'I made it myself,' said Millicent. 'It's carved from bison femur bone. Sorry. Do you hate it?'

'No,' said Ovid quickly.

'You're welcome to hate it.'

'I don't.'

'Did you say a bison femur bone?' enquired Uncle Harry.

'Millicent's dad is a butcher,' said Felicia.

'It's a Rare Meat Emporium,' said Millicent. 'Do you like it, Ovid?'

'Yes, very much.' He tried to sound convincingly grateful. It was not easy.

'It reminds me of you,' said Millicent.

'Because of the eyes?' asked Ovid.

'Because of the shell,' replied Millicent.

Gravity or
Foul Play?

Hazel had almost finished cleaning up the glass from the fallen chandelier when she caught her index finger on a sharp edge. She let out a small yelp, pulled her finger away and tasted the warm blood that sprang to the surface. She cursed herself for being so clumsy.

Nurse Griddle stepped into the room, demonstrating her uncanny ability to appear whenever an injury had occurred. She opened up her large medical bag and tutted. 'You really should be wearing gloves.'

'It's nothing.' Hazel put her hand behind her back. Her lifelong fear of the twins' nanny had not diminished since the discovery that Nurse Griddle was her biological mother. If anything, it had made her more fearful since Hazel now had the added concern that she had inherited Nurse Griddle's angular nose and pursed thin lips.

'I will be the judge of what is something and what is nothing.' Nurse Griddle took Hazel's hand. She examined it, then foraged inside her medical bag and pulled out a pair of tweezers, some antiseptic and a plaster.

'What happened to the chandelier?'

'It fell.'

'I can see that,' said Nurse Griddle. 'The question is, was it gravity or foul play?'

'I don't know, ma'am.'

'There is a piece of glass still inside the finger. Hold still now,' she said. 'This will hurt. But only momentarily.'

Nurse Griddle extracted the piece of glass with the tweezers, then squeezed a dollop of cream on the fingertip and stuck a plaster over the cut. She released Hazel's hand and looked at the plates of food on the table, each scene now decorated with broken glass. 'This is a rather ostentatious meal.'

'Yes, ma'am. Beaufort made it.'

'Beaufort?'

'He's Mr Marshall's personal chef.'

'Who is Mr Marshall?'

'Oh, please, call me Harry.'

Nurse Griddle turned to find Uncle Harry standing in the doorway. He made a small bow and offered his hand. 'Harry Marshall, the twins' long-lost uncle, at your service. You must be Nurse Griddle.'

She wrinkled her large nose and flared her nostrils. 'Hazel,' she said, maintaining eye contact but leaving Harry's hand unshaken, 'go and find some proper gloves so you can finish this job without incurring further injury.'

'Yes, ma'am.' Once Hazel was gone, Nurse Griddle spoke quietly but firmly. 'Why now?'

'I'm sorry?'

'Why come for them now?'

'I have already explained to the twins how I tried to keep in touch. It seems their old butler kept me at arm's length. Tom has been more reasonable. I remember him from their parents' wedding but I do not remember you.'

'I was not here then. I was taken on later as the twins' nanny.'

'Then you are to be congratulated. They have grown into a pair of fine young people.'

'And what have you grown into? From what I understand, your sister was the one who threw you out.'

Uncle Harry lowered his head in shame. 'It was a long time ago, but Ovid and Lorelli are still my family.'

'What do you want?' demanded Nurse Griddle. 'Don't tell me Heartless Harry has grown a heart.'

'Ah, so you read those kinds of newspapers, do you? Heartless Harry is a cruel nickname that owes more to pleasing alliteration than to the truth.'

'It refers to your business practices, does it not?'

'It does, and I will not deny that there are times when I have deserved it, but I am trying to be a better person. It's all any of us can do.'

'So you are here on some kind of journey of self-discovery. Is that it?'

'Something like that. I have a question for you. You servants all knew about me. May I ask why none of you told Ovid and Lorelli about me?'

'What should we have told them? That they have an incredibly wealthy uncle who has never once made any effort to see them?'

'That is hardly fair.'

'We are their guardians.' Nurse Griddle packed her things into the large medical bag. 'Tom and I will do anything to keep them from harm.'

'I promise you, I mean them no harm.'

'You haven't answered my question. Why have you come now?'

'I read about the fire.'

'The fire that occurred a year ago.'

Uncle Harry turned a plate of food around to admire Beaufort's scene. The shards of glass glistened like stars in the night sky. 'It took me time to build up the courage, but I owe it to Martha to reach out to them.'

'And here you are reaching out, with a personal chef and a reputation for ruthless business deals. What was that recent story about the zoo you shut down? Didn't you sell off those animals so that you could make money on the land?'

'That's not what happened,' snapped Uncle Harry. 'The conditions of that zoo were barbaric. I found good homes for every one of those animals. I saw to it myself, but that doesn't fit the Heartless Harry label so the press left out all those details.'

'Be that as it may,' said Nurse Griddle, 'I will be keeping a very close eye on you, Mr Marshall.'

'Then I will try to make your scrutiny worthwhile during my stay.'

'Your stay?'

'The twins have agreed to let me stay here for a few days.'

'How generous of them. Please remember that our job is to keep them safe from external harm.'

'What about internal harm?' asked Uncle Harry.

Nurse Griddle threw him a withering glance, then left.

Mr and Mrs Crick

Having been homeschooled all of their lives, Lorelli and Ovid had found Shelley Valley Secondary School a bewildering place. Ovid had immediately retreated into himself. Lorelli would have done the same had Felicia Crick not sat next to her on the first day and made Lorelli her friend. Lorelli was given no choice in the matter, but she was grateful. Having a friend she hadn't chosen was better than having no friend at all. Besides, she liked Felicia's world, in which everything was *wonderful* and *gorgeous* and *unimaginably divine*. It was a refreshing change and a sharp contrast to Lorelli's experience of life.

Felicia and Millicent followed Lorelli up to her bedroom at the top of the central spire of Thornthwaite Manor. Felicia kept making excited high-pitched noises about how elegant and magical and extraordinarily fabulous everything was. 'You must feel like Rapunzel,' she exclaimed as she entered the room.

'Rapunzel was a prisoner who needed a haircut,' said Millicent.

'Don't listen to old misery guts,' said Felicia, running from window to window. 'She's just upset because she has to work all week in that smelly old butcher's now her mum has run off.'

'It's not smelly, it's not a butcher's and she didn't run off. She just left.'

'That's the same thing, and if it's not smelly what is that smell on your hair?' said Felicia.

Seeing the hurt expression on Millicent's face, Lorelli turned to her and asked, 'Have you heard from your mother since she left?'

'No,' she responded timidly. 'She's dead to us now. That's what Dad says.'

'People can say upsetting things when they're feeling upset themselves,' said Lorelli kindly. She placed the statue on the south-facing windowsill, but Felicia picked it up and moved it to the one looking eastwards.

'This way,' said Felicia, 'it will catch the morning sun and fill your room with such splendid colours. It will be like waking up in a rainbow.'

Millicent adjusted the statue. 'We said it would be from both of us.'

'Yes, well,' said Felicia, 'Millicent helped design it, but it was my parents who made it so it's a bit more from me.'

Lorelli noticed a car parked on the driveway. 'Is that your parents, Felicia?'

'Yes, I think they wanted to have a nose. I'm not surprised. What a place. Oh, it's like living on top of the world up here.' Felicia picked up a fountain pen from Lorelli's desk.

Lorelli took it off her and put it back. 'You probably shouldn't leave them waiting too long,' she said, wishing Felicia would stop messing with her stuff.

'She wants us to go,' said Millicent.

'Not at all,' said Lorelli unconvincingly.

'What a lovely Lori-chicken you are,' said Felicia. 'But Millicent is right, we probably should be going.'

Lorelli led them back down to the car, where Mr and Mrs Crick were waiting. She had met them before when they had picked up Felicia from school and she had always been struck by how nice they seemed. They were always together and usually giggling about some private joke. Lorelli liked them a lot. She sometimes wondered if her own parents had been like that. She doubted it. The Cricks had a lightness of spirit that was absent from the Thornthwaites.

'Hello, Lorelli,' said Mrs Crick.

Mr Crick leaned over his wife. 'Did you like the statue?'

Mrs Crick pretended to bat him away.

'Very much, thank you,' said Lorelli.

'Good, that was my best work,' said Mr Crick.

'A-hem,' said Mrs Crick.

'Our best work then. You should drop by the shop one day. See how the other half live.'

'Honestly, Martin.' Mrs Crick placed a hand over her husband's mouth. He made Mm-mm noises as though trying to speak. 'He's right though,' she said. 'You should come. The workshop is lovely and warm at this time of the year.'

'Yes, I'd like that,' said Lorelli.

'I've a better idea,' said Felicia. 'Why don't Millicent and I come here for a sleepover one night this week? We could have ginger pop and gummy bears and stay up late.'

Lorelli knew about sleepovers and ginger pop from a series of old-fashioned books about a boarding school, but they had made no mention of gummy bears. Lorelli wondered if they were as dangerous as grizzly bears. She suspected not.

'My dad won't let me stay overnight,' said Millicent.

'How is your father?' asked Mrs Crick. 'Coping okay?'

'Yes,' said Millicent. 'He's fine. We're both fine. Dad says we're better off for cutting her out of our lives.'

'Give him our love,' said Mrs Crick.

Millicent didn't respond to this but Felicia piped up: 'A sleepover just the two of us then.'

'Felicia, love. You're being a little pushy,' said Mrs Crick.

'Felicia? Pushy? Surely not,' said Mr Crick.

'I'll let you know when it's a good day,' said Lorelli.

Mrs Crick started the engine. 'Come on then, you two, get in.'

The car wheels crunched over the gravel driveway as it pulled away. Lorelli turned around to see Ovid standing at the patio doors of the games room. Seeing her, he moved away, pretending he hadn't been watching.

The Willard Room

Uncle Harry found Tom in the garden, quietly muttering to the rose bush as he pruned it with a pair of secateurs that looked even older than him.

'Ah, Tom,' said Uncle Harry. 'I was wondering if you wouldn't mind giving me a hand with my bags. The twins have kindly said that I could stay with them in the manor for a few days.'

Tom lifted a white rose with his left hand, then very carefully clipped its stem with the ancient gardening tool.

'I didn't realise you were supposed to remove the actual roses,' said Uncle Harry.

'The thing about maintaining a healthy plant is that sometimes you must remove the older parts to allow the younger buds to blossom.' Tom revealed a smaller bud behind the large white rose.

'I'm afraid I've never had much time for nature,' said Uncle Harry. 'So these cases . . .'

Tom tucked his secateurs into his belt and wiped his hands on his trousers. He followed Uncle Harry up the lawn.

'You've lived here a long time, Tom,' said Uncle Harry.

'It's the only place I have ever called home,' he replied.

'Am I right in thinking that the twins are the third generation of Thornthwaites you've served?'

'Aye. Their grandfather, Silas, was my first master. He gave me this pair of snippers.' He tapped his secateurs. 'They still work as well as the day he gave them to me.'

They reached the car and Uncle Harry popped open the boot. Inside were two cases. One was extremely large, jet black and expensive-looking. The other was much smaller, faded green and worn at the edges. Tom reached to take the larger one.

'No, please,' said Uncle Harry. 'I'll carry my own luggage. I just need a hand with Beaufort's. He is in the kitchen busy in the fires of genius.'

'Your chef can stay in Mrs Bagshaw's old quarters,' said Tom. 'They are nearest the kitchen. You can have the Willard Room on the other side of the building.'

'Willard? Another distant relative?'

Tom nodded. 'Lord Willard lived in the early nineteenth century. The room has lovely views of Huxley Hill. The only downside is the poetry.'

'The poetry?'

'Willard believed himself to be a poet. His verses are carved into the walls of the room.'

'How interesting.'

Tom led the way to the stone steps in front of the house. 'It's not what you would call good poetry. I was all for papering over it but Dragos is keen to restore the house to its original state.'

'What's the poetry about?'

'His early ones are all about a girl he met at a fair, but the story goes that his mother didn't approve, so he was forced to marry another. Tragically, he never got over his first love. When he eventually died he was halfway through a poem about a man who murdered his wife . . .'

'Let me guess,' Uncle Harry interrupted. 'The poem was never finished because Willard was murdered by his own wife. I'm familiar enough with Thornthwaite history to know the recurring themes of irony and tragedy.'

'Not quite,' said Tom. 'Willard did indeed murder his wife, but unlike the hero of his poem he was caught and imprisoned. Plotting was never one of Willard's strong points.'

Uncle Harry shook his head sadly. 'With so much darkness in the twins' past, is it any wonder they are as they are?'

Tom paused at the top of the stairs. 'You see those trees at the top of that hill.' He indicated three leafless trees twisted and leaning the same way. 'Why do you reckon they are as they are?'

Uncle Harry looked up at the trees. 'I don't know. Some big storm? Or something to do with the prevailing wind or the position of the sun?'

'All fine guesses,' said Tom. 'But I've lived here all my life and those trees have always been like that. They are as they are because that's how they are.'

The Ivory Chess Set

Having grown up without modern technology, the Thornthwaite twins spent most evenings playing chess. Since the destruction of their previous metallic pieces, Ovid had found an ivory chess set in the attic. With Uncle Harry settling into his room, Ovid and Lorelli sat down in the games room to continue their match.

'It's my go, isn't it?' asked Lorelli.

'Yes, I moved my queen last.'

Lorelli assessed the board. She had lost the previous game so was determined to win this one. Over the years, she had found distraction to be the best way to force her brother into making a mistake. 'I think she likes you.'

'My queen?' replied Ovid.

Lorelli gave him a withering look. 'Millicent.'

'Why?'

'I have no idea. You're very annoying and you look like a discoloured goblin.'

'I mean why do you think that?'

'She looks at you for longer than most people can bear to.'

'Thank you,' said Ovid.

'You're welcome. Also, you are similarly melancholy.'

'Thank you.' Ovid considered this. 'Do you think she's like that because of her mother leaving?'

'I have no idea. Millicent doesn't get much of a word in with Felicia around. So, are you going to ask her out?'

'Felicia?'

'Millicent.'

'I don't know.'

Lorelli's hand hovered over her rook before a small smile in the corner of Ovid's mouth made her think better of it.

'I suppose I could invite her round to see my samurai sword collection or what's left of Aunt Gruoch's poison museum. Or I could take her to Devil's Leap.'

'Or you could do something normal people do, like take her to the cinema and then for a milkshake.' Lorelli moved her bishop forward, placing Ovid's knight in trouble.

'Predictable,' said Ovid.

'I think people like predictable things. They're safe.'

Ovid moved his pawn in between the bishop and the knight. 'I meant your move was predictable. What cinema?'

'They're showing films at the Memorial Hall every morning this week.'

They sat in silence for several minutes until Ovid said: 'I've got a killer move if you go where I think you're going to go.'

Lorelli was well accustomed to Ovid's tactic of talking over the game to force her into doing something silly. The obvious move was for her bishop to retreat, but Ovid knew that, so either he was trying to trick her into doing something else or he really did want her to go there and it was a double bluff. It was this kind of psychological game playing that made the average match last around six months.

'So . . . are you going to go?' said Lorelli at last.

'It's your turn.'

'I wasn't talking about chess.'

'Oh, that. I don't know. How do you know if you like someone enough to go on a date with them?'

'I think you go on a date to find out.' Lorelli moved the bishop back to its original point on the board.

'Ha. Back to square one.' Ovid picked up his bishop and took one of Lorelli's pawns. It was a bold move that opened up the floodgates to a cascade of carnage, which Lorelli already knew would wipe out half of the board and result in Ovid's ultimate advantage.

'I must say, you sound very knowledgeable on the subject of dates.' Ovid watched his sister closely for a reaction.

Lorelli stood up. 'Let's leave the game there for the night. I can't face all that destruction right now.'

Lorelli's Letters

Almost a year had passed since Lorelli had last seen Adam Farthing in the flesh. When he first arrived at Thornthwaite Manor he had drifted in like a warm summer's breeze, but he had left under a dark cloud of shame after the twins learned that he had conspired against them. Since then, he had written many letters to Lorelli, although none referred directly to that day. Thinking back on it, Lorelli found it difficult to recall precisely who had said what. Not that it really mattered. She continued to write to Adam because she felt it important to forgive him for plotting against Ovid and lying to her. If Adam Farthing could change, maybe she could too. Lorelli kept her ongoing correspondence a secret from her brother. Ovid had disliked Adam ever since he accidentally blew up their piano.

Adam's early letters had involved long, unwieldy, sprawling pages of messy writing. A confusion of thoughts bumped into each other and crashed off the ends of lines. The letters were hard to understand and filled with dark imagery that unnerved Lorelli.

Over time they had changed.

They were sparser, less elaborate and more restrained. Gone were the explosive adjectives and the long sentences.

In their place were short, clipped, carefully selected words. The handwriting was almost unrecognisably different. The letters now stood upright like soldiers. They were evenly spaced and regimented.

Lorelli opened the envelope carefully and pulled out the latest letter.

Dear Lorelli,

I am glad you received my last letter. It makes me happy to know you read my words. I am trying hard to be truthful in all I do. Doctor Mingus says I am making good progress. Sometimes we meet as a group. These are called Honesty Sessions. We all have to sit around and only say things that are true. It is hard. Sometimes we sit for a long time in silence. My truth partner says it's like listening to the cogs inside our heads as we try to work out what is true and what is not. I think that's right. Even writing this letter is taking me a long time because I have to stop in after every sentence to consider what to write next. But it is getting better. I am getting better. I hope I will be able to visit soon and you can see how much I have changed.

Yours,
Adam Farthing

Lorelli folded the letter and put it with the others in her top drawer. She wondered how she and Ovid would get on in an Honesty Session. The end of hostilities between them should have brought them closer together, but it felt like the opposite was true. Trying to kill each other had required each twin to show an interest in the other's movements. Why should Ovid care how Lorelli was planning to spend an afternoon, if he wasn't going to lay a complex trap to catch her.

Lorelli opened another drawer and pulled out a notepad and pen. She opened it up and started to write. She wrote:

The Tsar and the Dressmaker
By Lorelli Thornthwaite

Settled Dust

Hazel always rose early and got straight to work. Nurse Griddle had never been involved with the day-to-day housekeeping, so with Mrs Bagshaw gone it was down to Hazel to keep on top of the dusting and cleaning. She knew Lorelli would be swimming across Avernus Lake so she made her way up to clean her room. Lorelli enjoyed her early-morning swims but Hazel had no interest in stepping into the icy cold water that had claimed her father's life, especially as his body had never been recovered. With the dusting done, Hazel made her way down the spiral staircase, where she encountered Nurse Griddle on the landing.

'Hazel. What are you doing in Lorelli's room?'

'Cleaning, ma'am.'

'While she sleeps?'

'She has gone for a swim.'

'She is a reckless girl,' replied Nurse Griddle. 'How is your finger?'

'Better, thank you, ma'am,' said Hazel.

Nurse Griddle took the duster and polish from Hazel's hands. 'Cleaning products will only aggravate it.'

'Yes, ma'am. Sorry.'

'I am not telling you off. I am showing concern.'

'Yes, ma'am. Thank you.' Hazel curtsied.

'I have never been a naturally maternal person. Compassion and affection come easily to Mrs Bagshaw in a way that they simply do not to me.'

'Is that why you gave me away for Mrs Bagshaw to bring up, ma'am?'

Nurse Griddle acknowledged the impertinence of the question with a brief twitch of the lips. 'No. Not just like that. Your father died before you were born. When I first saw you, I looked into those hazel eyes of yours and all I could see was him. I could not bear it.'

'You gave me away because I looked like him?'

Nurse Griddle handed the duster and polish back to her. 'We cannot change the decisions we made in the past.'

'No, ma'am.'

An uncomfortable silence followed.

'You have plans for the day?' asked Nurse Griddle.

'I'm going to see my . . .' Hazel stopped herself saying the word *mum*. 'I'm going to see Mrs Bagshaw.'

'I see. I'm sure she appreciates your visits,' said Nurse Griddle. 'Would you like me to look after dinner preparation?'

'If you please, ma'am, Beaufort said he would cook.'

'Beaufort? Oh, the chef. I keep forgetting he is here too. What's he like, this French cook? I'm yet to meet him.'

'Chef, ma'am. He's wonderful, ma'am.'

'Wonderful?'

Hazel shrank under Nurse Griddle's gaze. 'I mean only that he is a good chef.'

'The word you used was wonderful.'

'His food tastes . . .' Hazel looked at her feet. 'He is a good chef, ma'am.'

'I'm sure he is, but what is he doing here? Why are either of them here?'

'Mr Marshall is the twins' uncle.'

'I am aware of that,' said Nurse Griddle impatiently, 'but he was their uncle last week and the one before. You see my meaning? Why would he turn up now?'

'I don't know, ma'am.'

'We need to keep an eye on him. And this *wonderful* chef of his. Remember, first and foremost it is our duty to protect our young masters. Thornthwaite Manor may be in a state of disrepair at the present moment, but these old bricks, and the land upon which they reside, amount to a vast inheritance.'

'Yes, ma'am. I have to go now. I must chop onions for Beaufort.'

'Onions? You should be thinking about what you want to do with your life. Don't limit yourself as I have done.'

'Yes, ma'am. I will think about that after I've chopped the onions.'

'You should be more your own person, Hazel. You're a capable girl. You owe it to yourself to follow your dreams.'

'Yes, ma'am.'

'Be more independent-minded.'

'I promise I will be. Please may I go now?'

'Yes.' Nurse Griddle sighed heavily. 'You may go.'

Water and Fire

With all the recent changes, Lorelli found it comforting to cling onto her old habits. Since the truce, trying to kill Ovid was no longer an option so she spent as much time as possible on other pursuits such as horse riding and enjoying dawn swims across Avernus Lake.

She had put on her swimming costume in the dark, grabbed a dressing gown and made her way down to the far side of the lake. It was bitterly cold as she got in but the sun was up by the time she was climbing out the other side. She felt that warming post-swim glow that made her skin tingle.

Thornthwaite Manor loomed in front of her. Its distinctive curved southerly towers were silhouetted against the morning sky. With so much in shadow, the only colour was the red tip of the central tower, lit by an early-morning sunbeam. It cast Lorelli's mind back to the great fire. Sometimes she wondered if it would not have been better if it had torn down the entire building. She looked up at her bedroom and imagined flames. She felt as though black clouds were closing in on the central spire. Her thoughts were so dark, it took her a moment to realise that these things were not in her head. It was real smoke. They were real flames. Her bedroom was on fire.

Lorelli broke into a run. Blood pounded in her ears as she ran full pelt across the dewy grass. She didn't notice Tom's lawnmower until he drew level with her and yelled, 'Hop on!'

She jumped on the back of the mower and he put his foot down. 'I was on my way to feed the horses when I saw it,' he said.

As they got closer, they saw that the flames were gone and the smoke was dissipating. Ovid, Hazel and Nurse Griddle had gathered on the steps outside the main entrance.

Tom stopped the lawnmower in front of the driveway and Lorelli jumped off. 'Where's everyone else?'

'Dragos and Harry are up there, trying to contain the fire,' said Ovid.

'What about Beaufort?' asked Lorelli.

Hazel said, 'He refuses to leave the kitchen because he is making crêpes, miss, and he says he would rather burn to death in the quest for perfection than escape with his life and a disappointing crêpe.'

'Ridiculous,' exclaimed Nurse Griddle. 'When I meet this man I will give him a piece of my mind.'

'This reminds me of that time I filled your teddy bear with paraffin,' said Ovid.

'Teddington never really recovered,' replied Lorelli.

Nurse Griddle looked at them sternly. 'I do hope we are not returning to those days.'

'This had nothing to do with me, if that's what you mean,' said Ovid. 'I was fast asleep.'

'Hazel, you were up there this morning,' said Nurse Griddle.

'It wasn't me, ma'am,' said Hazel.

'I meant, did you see anything that could have caused this?'

'No, ma'am.'

Dragos appeared at the door, closely followed by Uncle Harry wearing a pair of sooty pyjamas. Both men held fire extinguishers and smelt strongly of smoke.

'Well, that's one way to start the day,' said Uncle Harry.

'It is dangerous way,' said Dragos. 'It is lucky I put up fire alarms. Otherwise, this object would have burnt whole place to the ground.' Dragos held out Lorelli's glass statue.

'The statue? How?' she said.

'Refracted sunlight.' Ovid clicked his fingers.

'Yes,' said Dragos. 'It started fire on bed. You are lucky you were not there.'

'It works like a magnifying glass. The sunlight hits Lorelli's room around quarter to seven at this time of year,' said Ovid.

Lorelli turned to face him. 'You seem to know a lot about this.'

Ovid shrugged. 'I tried the same thing once. Don't you remember? You woke up to find Cowell's tail on fire?'

'Yes, I still have the claw marks in my neck. The poor thing was terrified,' said Lorelli.

'It did give a whole new meaning to the phrase "putting the cat out".' Ovid snorted with laughter and Lorelli smiled in spite of herself.

'I'm having trouble following you,' said Uncle Harry. 'Are you saying this has happened before?'

'They joke,' said Dragos sternly. 'They should not joke. Fire is no joking matter.' Dragos handed the statue to Lorelli. 'This is dangerous item. Where is it from?'

'It was a present from a friend,' said Lorelli.

'It is a dangerous present. I would not be calling this person friend,' stated Dragos.

'Is he always like this?' said Uncle Harry, winking at the twins. 'Come on, it was an accident. The twins aren't worried and it's hardly going to happen again.'

'This fire and the falling chandelier,' said Dragos. 'Too many accidents since you arrived.'

'I would be careful who you accuse of what,' said Uncle Harry. 'Now, shall we go and try these crêpes that my chef risked life and limb to make? I'll be driving to the village after breakfast if either of you would like a lift.'

Uncle Harry's Delahaye

The crêpes were magnificent. After breakfast, Uncle Harry brought his car around the front of the manor. Lorelli had never had any interest in cars but even she could appreciate Uncle Harry's vehicle. It was ostentatious yet classy. Old-fashioned but in perfect condition. The stripes were showy while the tinted windows made it totally private. Uncle Harry opened the driver's door and pulled the seat forward so that Ovid could climb into the back. He pushed the seat back and Lorelli got in the front.

'This is a million times better than the old banger Tom drives us around in,' said Ovid. 'I like the windows. It makes you feel cut off from everyone else.'

'The idea is to stop curious eyes.' Uncle Harry started the car. 'The problem is that when people can't see something they become even more obsessed with looking. Make it appear like you've got something to hide and everyone wants to know your business.'

'Have you got something to hide?' asked Ovid.

'Oh, lots.' Uncle Harry indicated left, then pulled out onto the main road towards Little Fledgling. 'You don't get to my position without picking up one or two enemies on the way.'

'Nurse Griddle said they call you Heartless Harry,' said Ovid.

'Some people do. And I doubt the journalist who came up with that stroke of genius earned half the money I donated to charities last year.'

'Why do they call you it?' said Ovid.

'Because it sells papers. I'm not saying I haven't been ruthless, but I've always had scruples.'

'She said you bought a zoo and then sold off all the animals,' said Ovid.

'Yes. In fact, that was one of the things that brought me here. It wasn't just any zoo. It was where your mother and I used to go when we were kids. Going back there brought back all those memories. Zoos are strange places. Martha and I, we loved all those animals, but as an adult it wasn't the animals I saw. It was the bars. It was the cages. They triggered a series of memories, which led me here, to this splendid cage of yours: Thornthwaite Manor. If anyone understands what it is to be imprisoned, it is you two.'

'Nurse Griddle doesn't trust you,' said Ovid.

'She is rightly very protective of you. All your servants are. It's no wonder. It's what they are paid to do. I'm family. Talking of which, I wonder if you wouldn't mind showing me the spot where my sister is buried once you have run your errands. I'd like to pay my respects.'

'Of course,' said Lorelli.

'Great. So who wants dropping where?'

'The library, please,' said Lorelli.

'The library?' Uncle Harry sounded surprised.

'Lorelli helps out there,' said Ovid. 'I'm going to the post office.'

'The library and the post office. What thrilling lives you both lead.'

Lorelli's Little Secret

As far as Ovid was concerned, once a week Lorelli helped out at Little Fledgling Library, where she put books back on shelves, organised displays and updated the database. Sometimes she went into great detail about the cataloguing system to avoid him learning the truth that she had persuaded the librarian, Miss Wilde, to help her write her novel. When Lorelli had first suggested it, Miss Wilde had refused. She said writing was impossible to teach, but Lorelli was determined to learn from the author of her favourite novel, *The Seven Dances of Franciska T~oth*, and eventually Miss Wilde gave in.

Lorelli found Miss Wilde sitting at a table, reading a book, wearing her usual colourful collection of mismatched clothes. Lorelli sat down and took out her notebook.

Miss Wilde looked up from her book. 'Lorelli,' she said vaguely, 'how are you getting on?'

'Good,' said Lorelli. 'I wrote four pages yesterday.'

'That sounds promising.' Miss Wilde closed her book. 'Are you still working on the one about the Victorian deep-sea diver?'

'No. I went off that one. This is a new one about a Russian dressmaker.'

Miss Wilde sighed and removed her glasses. 'I see.'

'Her dresses are so admired that the Tsar requests she make him a suit.' Lorelli loved the tingle of excitement she got from telling Miss Wilde about her stories. 'So the dressmaker makes this suit for the Tsar, although I don't know which one because I haven't researched that yet.'

'But you will, of course,' said Miss Wilde.

'Of course. So she has to go to measure the Tsar and they . . .'

'Fall in love?' interrupted Miss Wilde.

'Yes, but there's more. It turns out he's dying and he wants the suit because his body will be on display to the public.'

'Charming,' said Miss Wilde.

'You hate it,' said Lorelli.

'No. I don't hate it. It sounds like a good idea. Bleak, but then that is nothing new.'

'Then what?'

'I liked last week's idea about the deep-sea diver who got the bends on his wedding day and had to decide whether to go or not. I liked the one before that about the magician who was trying to make a potion that could make him forget his dead wife and the one about the scarecrow who fell in love with a crow. I like them all, Lorelli. Your ideas are rich, vivid and exciting.'

'Thank you.'

'But they are not stories. Not yet. They are single-cell organisms. They need to evolve. Instead, every week you come back with a new beginning. There is nothing wrong with starting books, but if you want to be a writer then you must learn to finish them.'

'Yes, but it has to be the right one.' Lorelli placed her pen on the table, making sure it was perfectly in line with the notepad.

Miss Wilde reached over the table and knocked the pen so that it was at an angle. 'Does it?'

Lorelli straightened the pen. 'Yes. There's no point finishing a story you're not a hundred per cent sure of.'

'I think there is a point for you,' said Miss Wilde. 'You are too concerned with perfection. Stories are imperfect things. They let you down. They wriggle away from your control. And sometimes you have to write short, ugly sentences just because sometimes, as a writer, you have to say short, ugly things. Non-poetic things. That is why it's called prose. My fear with you is that you begin a story and the moment it shows any sign of imperfection you give up and start a new one. If you want to progress you must stop striving for perfection and learn to finish something.'

'So I'll finish this one. As soon as I've researched that period in Russian history . . .'

'No.' Miss Wilde snatched Lorelli's pen and waggled it at her in frustration. 'No more delays. No more research. No more new ideas. Write your story, Lorelli.'

Lorelli was taken aback by Miss Wilde's stern words.

'I'm sorry.' Miss Wilde handed Lorelli her pen. 'It's just I've been under a lot of strain recently.'

'What's wrong?'

Miss Wilde held her gaze, momentarily lost for words. 'I . . . The library is up for sale.'

'For sale?'

'Yes, there have been cuts. There are always cuts.'

'But they can't sell the library.'

'Why not? Because people should have a right to access books whether or not they can afford to buy them? Because the benchmark of a civilised society is one that values learning and knowledge above profit? Because if we deny books to those who cannot afford them, we all become poorer?'

Lorelli felt a pang of guilt. She was anything but poor, and her reasons for objecting were entirely selfish. 'It's just . . . you can't not have a library,' she muttered.

'I'm afraid you can.'

'What will you do if it closes?'

'I don't know.' She stood up and placed her book back on the shelf. 'Perhaps I will take a leaf out of your book and write.'

'Oh yes. You could write a sequel to Franciska Tᵕoth,' said Lorelli.

Miss Wilde shook her head. 'Barely anyone read the first. Why would anyone want a second? But you should not worry about me. You must focus on your own passion. Do not put obstacles in your way. Other people will do enough of that for you. The only way to finish something is to start it.'

Ovid's Little Secret

As far as Lorelli was concerned her brother was going to the post office to pick up a parcel for Nurse Griddle. In truth, he was standing across the road from Hartwell's Rare Meat Emporium, peering through the grubby bus-stop glass at Millicent Hartwell. She was behind the counter, selling bison burgers, elk steaks, wild boar sausages and whatever else her father had in stock that week.

It was Ovid's third time spying and he had never seen either Millicent or her father smile. Mr Hartwell was a large man with a bald head and a bulldoggish face. He had a habit of wiping his hands on his white overalls, so there were diagonal red stains around his large belly. Millicent wore matching overalls but hers were spotless. Ovid had seen Mrs Hartwell on his first visit, but since then it was always Millicent who dealt with the customers. Mr Hartwell spent most of his time in the back room, cutting, chopping, dicing and mincing. Millicent was standing as still as a statue in the empty shop when Uncle Harry entered. Ovid shifted to get a better position but a bus stopped in front of him, blocking his view. Its brakes hissed and the doors slid open.

'Master Thornthwaite,' said the driver. 'Hop on then.'

'I'm not here for the bus, thank you,' replied Ovid.

'Why are you waiting at a bus stop then?'

'You can stand at a bus stop without waiting for a bus.'

'You can indeed. But why would you?'

'That's not really any of your business.'

The driver chuckled. 'I'm not scheduled to leave for another two minutes, so if you're staying here, you're staying here with me.'

'Can't you leave early?'

'Could do.' The driver pulled out a rolled-up newspaper from beside his seat. 'But when you leave early, people who know the timetable, which most people do around here, get awful irate with old Dickie here because they like to leave things to the last minute. No, it's not worth the hassle to leave early.'

'That's fascinating . . .'

'Yes, everyone knows everyone around here. You're the third generation of Thornthwaites I've known. I remember your grandfather, Silas. He was a mean old soul. He used to come round the village himself on rent day. Didn't trust his servants not to pocket the payments, you see.'

'Yes, I'd heard that . . .' said Ovid.

'I even went to your parents' wedding. That was quite a day. Your father certainly didn't inherit old Silas's meanness. I've never seen such a do.'

'You knew my parents?'

'Not especially, but, see, your old man didn't have many friends so he hired a bunch of us from the village to sit on his side of the church.'

Ovid understood how pathetic it sounded that his father had to hire guests for his own wedding, but he was hardly swimming in friends himself.

'I actually got picked to be an usher,' continued the bus driver. 'I would have said no but he paid extra for ushers and I was saving up to impress a girl.'

'Are girls impressed by money then?'

'Some are. This one wasn't, as it happened. She went off with a fella by the name of Artie Newly who didn't have a penny to his name.' Ovid was unsure why the bus driver had decided to give him his life story, but he was showing no signs of stopping. 'You know her, I believe. Eileen Griddle. She works up the manor now.'

'Nurse Griddle?' said Ovid.

He nodded. 'Only Artie died when . . .'

'He drowned in the lake,' said Ovid. 'Yes, I know this story. He got drunk and bet his friend he could swim across the lake fastest.'

'And have a guess who that other man was.' The bus driver pointed at himself. 'Yours truly.'

'You?'

'Yes. I won the bet, Eileen lost her fiancé and I lost any chance of winning her over. She upped and left on the day he died, you see. I met my wife shortly after that and moved on. That's the thing, you see – young hearts break easily enough, but they do mend in time. Oh, talking of time . . .'

The bus doors shut and the bus noisily drove away. Before Ovid could dive for cover, Millicent looked up and spotted him. He stared back, unsure what to do. She raised a hand

61

in a kind of half-wave. Ovid fought the urge to turn tail and run. He forced himself to cross the road. Millicent was alone in the shop, but when Ovid opened the door he could hear Mr Hartwell out the back, hacking away at a piece of meat.

'Hello, Ovid,' said Millicent quietly.

'I was waiting for the bus,' Ovid said.

'I think you missed it.'

'Yes.' Ovid wished he could walk out and come back in again.

'Your uncle was just here.'

'Right.'

The silence between them felt like a brick wall. The longer he went without speaking, the higher it grew. Ovid needed to say something. Anything.

'Thank you for my present,' he said at the same time that Millicent was saying, 'Did you have a nice birthday?'

'Yes, thank you,' said Ovid over Millicent saying, 'You're welcome.' The silence returned until Millicent broke it with, 'Your uncle told me about the fire. He said it was Felicia's statue.'

'Yes. Stupid accident really.'

A brief but unmistakable look of fear flashed in Millicent's eyes. 'Was it?'

'What do you mean?'

'Nothing. I'm sorry. I shouldn't have said anything. You're right. It was an accident.'

As strange and awkward a conversation as it was, it had broken the ice. In the back, Mr Hartwell switched on the mincing machine.

'I was wondering if you would like to go to see a film with me,' said Ovid. 'There's one on at eleven at the Memorial Hall tomorrow.'

The mincing machine stopped chugging halfway through Ovid's question and he realised he was shouting.

'Yes,' whispered Millicent.

'Really?' Ovid had been unprepared for the possibility of Millicent saying yes.

'You can buy the tickets,' she said. 'I'll see you there. You'd better go now.'

Ovid's face was not naturally given over to expressions of joy, but he couldn't help himself as he walked away. Not only had he just asked Millicent Hartwell out. She had said yes.

Martha Thornthwaite's
Headstone

When Lorelli met Ovid on the bridge she was unnerved by the smile on his face. Her brother had a number of smiles, all with different meanings. There was his devilish grin, his sly smirk and his determined grimace. This was new. If she wasn't mistaken, Ovid was happy.

'I told Uncle Harry we'd meet him by the church,' he said.

'So, what do you think? Is he genuine?' replied Lorelli.

'Of course. Tom recognised him from our parents' wedding and Nurse Griddle has seen his picture in the paper,' said Ovid.

'That isn't what I mean,' said Lorelli. 'Don't you get the feeling he's hiding something?'

'Everyone hides things,' said Ovid.

They walked along the side of the river to Little Fledgling's crumbling old parish church. Uncle Harry's car was parked outside.

'What a lovely day for a walk in a cemetery,' said Ovid, with unusual lightness of tone.

'Right, that's it. What *are* you so happy about?' asked Lorelli.

'Being happy isn't a sin.'

A voice from behind said: 'The Thornthwaite twins should know a thing or two about sin.'

The twins turned to see Father Whelan's bald head poking around the side of the heavy wooden door.

'Sin attracts sin. I saw you.' He pointed a crooked finger at Ovid. 'I saw you at the butcher's shop.'

'Butcher's shop?' said Lorelli.

'I went to pick up an order for the kitchen,' said Ovid hastily. 'What's so sinful about a butcher's shop?'

'Mrs Hartwell mysteriously vanishes,' said the wild-eyed priest. 'Her husband specialises in rare meat. Where, pray, do you think that meat comes from?' He lowered his voice and hissed, 'He's serving his wife up as steak.'

'We don't want to hear your stories,' said Lorelli.

Father Whelan was well known for concocting conspiracies and spreading outrageous accusations about his parishioners.

'That's right. Leave us alone,' said Ovid.

'Reject your sinful ways!' he cried. 'Wash yourselves clean of your lies. You are not beyond redemption, but you must repent.'

Father Whelan slammed the door shut and the twins continued towards Uncle Harry's car.

'Crazy old fool,' muttered Ovid.

'So where is this meat you picked up?' asked Lorelli.

'It wasn't in yet,' he replied. 'Listen, Uncle Harry's on the phone.'

They drew level with the car. Uncle Harry was inside talking.

'So I'll action the sale today. It will be mine by the morning . . . Yes, I mean yours . . . Yes, I am buying it for you but it will be in my name . . . I promise I won't interfere. You know your side of the business. I know my place . . . I've told you. It will be clearly stated that when I am gone the whole place is yours. In the meantime, I will be the most silent of partners. No interference. Yes, I'll see you later on.'

Uncle Harry opened the car door and stepped out. 'Oh, hello, you two,' he said. 'I didn't hear you.' He dropped his phone into his jacket pocket.

'Business call?' said Ovid.

'Yes, property acquisition as usual,' replied Uncle Harry. 'So shall we go then?'

Lorelli led the way. Little Fledgling cemetery was a bleak place during the winter months, but at this time of year the trees and plants were blooming and budding. The elaborate Thornthwaite gravestones were tucked away in the far corner.

'It must feel like a terrible burden,' said Uncle Harry as they made their way along the winding path.

'What must?' asked Lorelli.

'This heritage. All these lords and ladies that went before you, the expectations people have for you . . . your legacy. When your mother and I were children no one expected us to become anything. We were poor but we were free. I can't imagine how weighed down you must feel.'

Neither twin knew what to say, so they said nothing at all.

'I say, isn't that your builder?' said Uncle Harry.

There was no one else in the cemetery so the broad-shouldered figure in the yellow hard hat stood out. Dragos was kneeling down in the middle of the Thornthwaite plot. Spotting them approach, he got to his feet.

'Young masters,' he said, 'it is good to see you.'

'What are you doing here?' asked Lorelli.

'Come to pay your respects, I dare say,' said Uncle Harry.

Dragos turned to face him. He placed his right hand on a gravestone in the shape of Thornthwaite Manor. 'This is Lord Christof's headstone,' he said. 'I use this for reference for restoration.'

'You are using a gravestone as a blueprint,' said Uncle Harry. 'A rather apt metaphor.'

'It is not metaphor. It is gravestone.' Dragos pulled the visor on his cap down, to shield his eyes from the glare of the sun. 'Lord Christof built this gravestone as model. All other designs burnt in the great fire. There is no more meaning than that.'

'Lord Christof, 1832 to 1867.' Uncle Harry read the words etched into the stone. 'Such short lives, always such short lives.'

'Is he the one who added the sloping towers?' asked Ovid.

'Yes, though they were supposed to be straight,' said Lorelli. 'Christof wasn't a very good architect. Every other building he designed fell down. He threw himself off one of the towers in the end.'

'Irony and tragedy,' muttered Uncle Harry as he crouched down in front of a plain black stone with three names carved out.

Lord Silas Thornthwaite
1908–1959

Lady Mabel Thornthwaite
1918–1953

Lady Agnes Thornthwaite
1926–1971

'Looks like this one had two wives,' Uncle Harry said.

'I have no interest in this history beyond that of the old lady,' said Dragos. 'I will go now. Young masters, good day.'

Dragos walked briskly away and Lorelli turned to Uncle Harry.

'Lord Silas Thornthwaite was our grandfather,' explained Lorelli. 'His first wife died in a gas explosion, so he married again.'

'These are such dark stories for children,' said Uncle Harry, shaking his head. 'How do you even know all this?'

'Our old head butler wrote a history of the family,' said Lorelli. 'According to that, Lord Silas died in the same place a few years later.'

'So they both perished in the same mine?' said Uncle Harry.

'Did I mention a mine?' asked Lorelli.

Uncle Harry stood up. 'No, you said gas explosion. I assumed mine. So where is Martha's headstone?'

Lorelli looked at her brother to see if he had registered Uncle Harry's sudden change of subject, but he had stopped in front of their parents' gravestone. 'This is the one.'

Uncle Harry's naturally casual manner vanished as he dropped to his knees in front of it. With his head bowed, he raised a hand to the stone and felt its coldness.

'Martha,' he whispered, 'I'm sorry, sis. I let you down, but I'm going to make it up to you . . .'

'How did you let her down?' asked Lorelli.

'I made her a promise.' Uncle Harry closed his eyes and whispered, 'I promised her that if anything happened to her, I would look out for you. I have not lived up to my word. I hope it's not too late.'

'We don't need looking after,' said Ovid.

Uncle Harry nodded. 'I know. Still, I must do right by her. You must allow me to try.'

'Try to do what?' asked Ovid.

He offered them his open palms. Unsure what to do, they took one each. His hands were warm as he closed his fingers around their wrists. 'Lorelli, Ovid, with your permission I want to write you into my will.'

'Your will?' repeated Ovid.

'I want to show you how serious I am. I want my entire wealth to be divided equally between you when I die.'

Lorelli and Ovid exchanged a glance, then Ovid said, 'And is dying something you plan on doing any time soon?'

Uncle Harry smiled. 'Always so direct. No, it is not. I want to get to know you first, if that's all right with you. I want to be an uncle to you. I want to make it up to you. And to Martha. You are only half Thornthwaite. The other half is the same blood as mine. So what do you say? Will you be my heirs?'

'That's very generous of you,' said Lorelli.

'No. It's the right thing to do. You are my family. I understand that now.' He touched the top of the gravestone gently, feeling its rough edge. 'And to think I really thought it would just feel like a block of stone.'

Clairmont Prison

Hazel left Tom Paine in the car park while she went into the low-security prison. She found Mrs Bagshaw sitting in the visitors' room, knitting. The plump cook looked more like a patient waiting to see the doctor than a convicted murderer in a prison.

'Hello, Hazel dear.' She put the knitting down and stood to embrace her. 'How kind of you to pop by. Have they made you a cup of tea?' She glanced at the unsmiling guard in the corner of the room and made a 'T' sign with her hands. The guard did not respond.

'I'm fine, thank you,' said Hazel. 'What are you knitting?'

'A new scarf. My neck does get awfully stiff after an afternoon in the garden with my turnips. It's funny, before I came here I was never much of a one for gardening. Nowadays, my vegetable garden is a little oasis. It's a place where I can really escape from all this. I'm planning to make a soup when this crop's ready. But listen to me prattling on. You need to tell me your news. How did the birthday cake turn out?'

'It was not as good as yours.'

Mrs Bagshaw chuckled. 'You must all be missing my cooking while I'm in here. What are you missing most? My apple dumplings or my sheep-bone stew?'

'It's difficult but we are all fine.'

'That's good to hear.' Mrs Bagshaw leant forward. 'So no more . . . you know . . . incidents involving the young masters?'

'Only the chandelier, but that was a loose fitting. Oh, and the fire in Lorelli's bedroom, but that was an accident.'

Mrs Bagshaw looked at the guard, then whispered, 'Are you sure?'

'Yes. Mr Marshall said there were no signs of anything untoward.'

'Marshall?'

'Harry Marshall.'

'Oh dear, oh dear.' Mrs Bagshaw shook her head. 'Why has he come back after all these years?'

'Have you met him then?'

'Yes. On Lord and Lady Thornthwaite's wedding day. He had a big row, shouted all sorts of unpleasant things, as I recall. He had to be escorted out.'

'A row about what?'

'He wasn't so keen on the twins' mother marrying Lord Thornthwaite. He thought it would end badly. I suppose he was right, wasn't he? But Mr Crutcher never let him near the twins after their parents passed away. God rest their souls.'

Hazel thought it best to steer the conversation away from the death of the twins' parents since Mrs Bagshaw was in prison for the murder of Lord Thornthwaite. The truth was much more complicated than that but it hardly mattered now. The judge had reached his verdict and Mrs Bagshaw was serving her sentence. What did it matter whom she had really poisoned?

'Why did you never tell Ovid and Lorelli they had an uncle?'

Mrs Bagshaw developed a sudden interest in her knitting. 'Sorry, Hazel. I've come to a tricky bit. I need to concentrate.'

'I didn't know there were tricky bits on scarves.'

Mrs Bagshaw put down the knitting needles. 'Why would he turn up after all this time?'

'I believe he's looking for a family.'

Mrs Bagshaw took Hazel's hands and pulled her close. 'Family is important. The thought of you is what keeps me going in here.'

'I wish you were back home,' said Hazel.

'You've got Nurse Griddle. Honestly, you'd think one mother would be enough for anyone.' The sadness in her eyes gave lie to the cheeriness of her tone. 'And it won't be long before I'm back with you, I'm sure.'

'The judge gave you a fourteen-year sentence.'

'Yes, but the prison governor hasn't yet tasted my turnip soup. I'll bet he'll look on my case with very different eyes after he's been won over by my soup. Oh yes, these turnips are my ticket out of here.'

No Prestige
in Obscurity

All the servants had rooms in the northwestern quarter of the manor, except Tom Paine who had a cottage in the grounds. With Mrs Bagshaw in prison and Alfred Crutcher dead, the servants' quarters were very quiet, so Nurse Griddle was surprised to find the bathroom door locked. She rattled the handle to make sure it wasn't jammed.

"Ello?' cried a voice from within. 'There is someone in 'ere.'

'Who is that?' responded Nurse Griddle.

'My name is Beaufort Nouveau,' he replied. 'I am the chef.'

'Oh, yes, Mr Marshall's cook.' Nurse Griddle could tell from his voice what kind of man he was. Arrogant, idiotic and overconfident. Everything she hated in a man. 'May I ask what you are doing here, Mr Nouveau?'

'I do not think that is any of your business, but if you must know I am maintaining the integrity of my moustache.'

'I did not mean what are you doing in the bathroom. I am enquiring why you are here at Thornthwaite Manor,' she said. 'Surely a world-renowned chef such as yourself should be working in a restaurant. There is no prestige in obscurity.'

'I 'ave 'ad prestige,' said Beaufort. 'I have wowed food critics around the world with my creations, but it is time for me to be my own man. In the end, a restaurant chef is a wage slave and no better than a lowly dishwasher. Mr Marshall is 'elping me realise my goal.'

'Well, while you are staying here, may I suggest you use the bathroom at the far end of the corridor? It is nearer your own quarters.'

'If it means I can be left alone to my personal grooming, I certainly will. Good day, *madame*.'

'Good day.' Nurse Griddle swivelled on a heel and stormed off to use the other bathroom. She did not like Uncle Harry or his arrogant chef. She didn't know what the twins were thinking, inviting them to stay. It worried her profoundly.

Nurse Griddle was not accustomed to change. She had avoided it whenever possible, but ever since the great fire life at Thornthwaite Manor had felt worryingly different. She didn't like it at all. The twins' truce meant she had far fewer injuries to keep her occupied. Their decision to attend Shelley Valley Secondary School meant she no longer had lessons to plan. Nurse Griddle had found herself with increasingly more time on her hands.

After availing herself of an alternative bathroom, she went to the library, pulled out a book and sat down to read. She was a quick reader and had got as far as chapter three when she realised she had read the book before. She closed it and gazed out of the window. A large unmarked white van was turning around. Nurse Griddle replaced the book and made her way to the entrance. She opened the front door but the van was driving away.

'Hello!' she called out.

The van did not stop.

She didn't know why she was so jittery today. It was not uncommon for drivers to take the turning that led to the manor by mistake. She listened to the van's engine drive away. She envied the driver's ability to turn around and leave so easily. Nurse Griddle had made one decision when she was much younger that had led her down the path to Thornthwaite Manor. She had spent the rest of her life living with the consequences of that decision. Sometimes she wished she could turn things around so easily.

An Invitation

Uncle Harry wanted to take a longer walk around the cemetery, so Lorelli and Ovid returned to the car to wait for him. Ovid was still alarmingly cheerful. Lorelli caught him humming, but it wasn't one of the dirges he liked to play on the harpsichord. It was a disturbingly light, happy tune.

'So?' she said. 'Why is he putting us in his will?'

'Maybe he's telling the truth. Have you thought about that?'

'There's definitely something up with you today,' said Lorelli.

'I just think we should give him a chance.' Ovid grinned. 'We're not exactly swimming in relatives.'

When they reached Uncle Harry's car Lorelli spotted Felicia sitting on a wall, wearing a red bonnet and a poufy dress. Seeing them, she hopped off the wall and ran over to throw her arms around Lorelli.

'Lori-chicken!' she squawked. 'I knew it would be you. I saw the car go past the shop and I said to myself, that's Uncle Harry's car. It's such a wonderful-looking thing. Doesn't it just scream glamour and wealth?'

'Now, is that the same screaming as when one's bedroom is on fire, I wonder?' Ovid sniggered.

'What are you talking about?' asked Felicia.

'It's supposed to be a joke except it's not funny,' explained Lorelli.

'Whereas having your bedroom set on fire by a glass statue of you is hilarious,' said Ovid.

Felicia gasped. 'What fire? Lori-chicken, what's he talking about?'

'It was just an accident,' said Lorelli.

'Oh, how awful, and it's my fault.' Felicia held her hand up to her mouth in shock. 'I should have known, and to think it was me who insisted on putting it where I knew the sun would come up. What must you think of me?'

'Don't be silly,' said Lorelli. 'I know it was an accident. Ovid's just got a twisted a sense of humour.'

'Oh yes, I'm terribly twisted,' said Ovid. 'So what's for her next birthday? Poisoned banana cake? Deadly lip gloss? An exploding jewellery box?'

Felicia peered at him closely. 'You are a very strange boy,' she said.

'He's an idiot,' said Lorelli.

'Oh, but the thought of ever hurting you,' said Felicia. 'It would be like hurting myself.'

'Two for the price of one,' said Ovid. 'Sounds fun.'

'Ovid, stop it.' Lorelli was getting annoyed. 'Felicia, why don't you come for that sleepover tonight?'

'Tonight? Oh, yes. How wonderful.' Felicia clapped her hands together excitedly. 'We can go riding on your horses, toast marshmallows and tell each other our secrets.'

'Yes, that sort of thing,' said Lorelli uncertainly.

Ovid gave his sister a knowing look. 'All of your secrets?'

She scowled at him, then said to Felicia: 'We can take you now if you like.'

'Oh, Lori-chicken,' chirruped Felicia. 'That would be heaven in a basket, but I have to pack and prepare. I'll have my mother drop me round this afternoon. It will be so much more thrilling than hanging around this dead-end village.'

The Alteration of the Will

Bernard Farthing, the twins' lawyer, was a large man, uncomfortable with the amount of space he took up in most circumstances. Standing in the grand hallway of Thornthwaite Manor, under Nurse Griddle's scrutinising gaze, he was melting like a slug in salt. 'Mr Farthing. What brings you here?' she asked.

'I received a call from a Mr Harry Marshall? He said he had some business regarding a will.'

'I see. And, tell me, has your son Adam joined you?'

'No. I'm not sure he's ready to come back here yet.'

'Last time he was here, his lies and deceit caused a great deal of mischief,' said Nurse Griddle.

Mr Farthing coughed self-consciously. 'That is in the past. I would rather we didn't dredge up such unpleasantness again. My son is seeing a specialist about his problem. Doctor Mingus has an excellent track record. She says she is making good progress renewing his relationship with the truth.'

'Does that mean he has stopped lying?' asked Nurse Griddle bluntly.

Mr Farthing cleared his throat. 'He's certainly getting a lot better.'

The sound of tyres on gravel and slamming car doors preceded the arrival of Ovid, Lorelli and Uncle Harry.

'I will leave you to your business then,' said Nurse Griddle, returning to the library.

Lorelli was the first through the door, but Ovid and Uncle Harry were close behind. 'Mr Farthing?' she said. 'What are you doing here?'

'I called him,' said Uncle Harry. 'I wanted to show you how serious I am, so I contacted your lawyer to make the alteration to my will.'

'That was quick work,' said Ovid.

'I do work quickly,' replied Uncle Harry. 'Procrastination is for the unambitious. Time-wasting is a waste of time.'

'I'm very pleased to meet you,' said Mr Farthing. He went to shake hands with Uncle Harry but his elbow knocked a plant pot on a porcelain plinth. Lorelli steadied it.

'And you,' said Uncle Harry. 'Now, to business. I have asked you here to help me make Ovid and Lorelli the sole beneficiaries of my wealth and assets. My property, yachts, jets, cars, helicopters, island and vast amounts of money. All of it, in the eventuality of my death, is to be split between them equally.'

Mr Farthing anxiously rummaged through his pockets to find a pen, but when he did it slipped through his fingers. He tried to catch it and somehow managed to fling it across the hall.

'Perhaps we should find a room to sit down and go through the details,' said Uncle Harry. 'Ovid, shall we find a suitable room?'

'Certainly.'

Mr Farthing and Lorelli followed Ovid and Uncle Harry down a corridor. Mr Farthing spoke quietly to Lorelli. 'I believe you maintain a correspondence with my son.'

Lorelli checked Ovid was not listening before whispering, 'I reply to his letters, yes.'

'And his letters, do they . . . I mean, are they wholly . . . you know. How does he seem to you?'

'As far as I can tell, they are truthful,' said Lorelli. 'He said he was seeing a new specialist.'

'Yes, Doctor Mingus. Her techniques seem to be working.'

'Whose techniques seem to be working?' asked Ovid.

'Mr Farthing was telling me about a book on chess techniques,' lied Lorelli.

'Oh really? What's it called?'

'I, er . . . I forget the title,' said Mr Farthing.

'It's going to take more than a book for you to claw back our current game,' said Ovid.

'Talking of games, how about this room?' said Uncle Harry.

They all went into the games room and Mr Farthing sat down at the table. Ovid, Lorelli and Uncle Harry remained standing. Mr Farthing opened his briefcase and pulled out a fountain pen and a pad of paper. 'So, Mr Marshall, do you have any other family?'

'None,' said Uncle Harry.

'No children?'

'Sadly not.'

'Wife?'

'Also sadly not.'

'Ex-wife?'

'Less sadly not. No, mine has been an isolated existence, but I hope to change all that now.'

'If that is the case then it shouldn't be too complicated,' said Mr Farthing. 'I can draw up a draft version of the will, naming Ovid and Lorelli as beneficiaries of your estate, then bring it back for you to sign next week.'

'Or tomorrow,' said Uncle Harry, placing a firm hand on the lawyer's shoulder. 'I pay extra for speed.'

'Tomorrow should be possible,' said Mr Farthing.

'Good. I never waste time in matters of business. I see no reason why I should do so in matters of the heart.'

The Fortune of Family

Hazel was the only member of the household to ever visit Mrs Bagshaw. She knew the others had their reasons for staying away, but she did sometimes wish they would show more interest.

'Back home then?' said Old Tom as she climbed into the passenger seat of his rusty old car.

'Yes, please,' said Hazel.

Tom put the car into reverse, then navigated his way out of the car park.

'She's started growing turnips,' said Hazel.

Tom kept his eyes fixed on the road and both hands rigidly clutching the steering wheel. 'Turnips,' he said. 'That's good.'

'And she's knitting a scarf.'

'Surprised they allow knitting needles in prisons . . .'

'It's a low-security prison.'

'There you are then.'

Tom continued to drive in silence until Hazel spoke again. 'Why do you never ask after her?'

Tom considered the question before answering. 'I suppose it's the same reason that I've never watered the crocuses on the south slopes. You see, that's the lovely thing about crocuses. They open up whether you water them or not, so what's the point in watering them?'

It was a typical Tom response. Hazel had once asked him if he cared more about plants than people. He had responded, 'Not more. I'd say I care about the same for the people and plants in my life.'

When they finally reached the manor, Tom dropped her off outside the kitchen before parking the car in the garage. She went straight to the kitchen, where Beaufort was busy crushing a piece of ginger with a large knife.

'Where 'ave you been? I 'ad to de-stone my own olives this morning.'

'I told you, I was visiting Mrs Bagshaw.'

'The one in prison. Yes, you did tell me. 'Ow was it? It cannot be easy for you seeing 'er like that.'

Hazel was unsure how to respond. None of the others had ever asked her about her feelings before. 'I'm fine,' she said.

'Good. Then you will next be needed in one hour's time. Until then, your time is your own.'

'If you please, chef, I'd like to observe,' said Hazel.

He squinted at her, then returned his attention to the ginger. 'You may remain on two conditions. One, you do not ask me silly questions. Two, you do not get under foot.'

'*Oui*, chef.'

Beaufort grunted, then got back to crushing the ginger. Watching him work was the single most exciting experience of Hazel's life. She loved the way he glided from workspace to hob and back again with the elegance of a ballet dancer, the precision of a soldier and the flamboyant confidence of a matador. When Uncle Harry informed him that Felicia Crick would be joining them for dinner, Beaufort responded with an explosion of wildly gesticulated French before he calmed down and got on with it.

As dinnertime neared, Beaufort sent Hazel to set the table and ensure the guests were in 'the right frame of mind' for dinner. Hazel was not entirely sure what this meant but she did as she was told unquestioningly. At eight o'clock they carried in four pies that looked like miniature gothic castles of pastry, complete with gargoyles and turrets. Hazel and Beaufort placed them on the table, then Beaufort took a small gravy jug and carefully poured the scalding-hot liquid into the tops of the towers so that it gushed out of the gargoyles' mouths.

Ovid, Lorelli and Uncle Harry stared in astonished admiration. Felicia clapped her hands and whooped.

'It's like magic,' she said.

'It's quite a pie,' said Ovid.

'Pie,' said Beaufort. 'Such a tiny little word! Pie. From the Latin *pica*, meaning magpie. And just as the eponymous bird, a pie must gather found treasures to create something new. I call it my Divine Pie, named after the great poet Dante's vision of hell. You see, there are nine levels to this pie.'

'It's amazing,' said Lorelli.

'Should we work down or up?' asked Uncle Harry.

'An artist cannot dictate how one should consume his art. Some want to travel down, plunging into the depths of each rich layer. Others prefer to find out what is at the bottom first.'

'What about those who just want to mess everything up?' said Ovid.

'Ah, yes, the lovers of chaos,' said Beaufort. 'All are equal in the art of food. Now, please excuse 'Azel and myself. We must go prepare the dessert. Come 'Azel.'

'*Oui*, chef.'

Beaufort's Divine Pie was so delicious it even silenced Felicia. No one spoke until the final mouthfuls had been swallowed.

'That. Was. Amazing,' said Felicia at last.

'The man is a genius.' Uncle Harry picked up a napkin to dab a droplet of gravy from his chin.

'It wasn't bad,' said Ovid.

'Not bad at all,' agreed Lorelli.

'Does Hazel never dine with you?' asked Uncle Harry.

'Of course not,' said Felicia. 'Servants should be as useful and silent as the furniture. Isn't that right, Lori-chicken?'

'No. It's not like that,' said Lorelli. 'But no. She eats . . .' She realised she had no idea when or where Hazel ate.

'It's just as it should be,' said Felicia. 'Oh, to live like this, it's an absolute dream.'

'Oh yes, our life is so dreamy,' said Ovid, rolling his eyes.

Lorelli tried to ignore him. 'I envy you, Felicia,' she said. 'You have parents.'

'I'd rather have servants than parents any day,' said Felicia. 'Servants do what you tell them. Parents tell you what to do.'

'Funnily enough, we were never given the choice,' said Ovid.

'So, Lorelli,' said Uncle Harry in a blatant attempt to move the conversation on, 'I take it Felicia will be sleeping in your room tonight.'

'No,' said Lorelli. 'My room is still a little smoky. We'll be in the Gruoch Suite in the west wing.'

'The Gruoch Suite,' repeated Felicia. 'What a wonderful name.'

'It was named after Lady Gruoch Thornthwaite,' said Lorelli. 'She lived here in the early nineteenth century.'

'Was she the one with the older sister who was supposed to marry Lord Allegro?' asked Ovid.

'That's right. Gwendoline,' said Lorelli.

'What happened?' asked Felicia.

'The older sister died on the night of her engagement. The father offered Gruoch as a back-up.'

'How romantic,' said Felicia.

'How is *that* romantic?' asked Ovid.

'Marriages are always romantic,' said Felicia defensively.

'The sister died,' said Ovid.

'Everyone is dead in history,' said Felicia. 'What does it matter how it happened?'

'History is all about the how,' said Uncle Harry. 'Talking of which, I'd love to see that book you mentioned.'

'Alfred's Crutcher's history of our family?' said Lorelli. 'There's a copy in the library.'

'I'll be sure to take a look,' said Uncle Harry. 'Now, may I propose a toast?'

Ovid, Lorelli and Felicia raised their glasses of dark berry juice. Uncle Harry lifted his glass of red wine. 'To true fortune,' he said. 'The fortune of family.'

'The fortune of family,' repeated the others.

Flush of Death

After dinner, Uncle Harry announced he was taking a late walk. Ovid went to his room while Lorelli took Felicia to the Gruoch Suite. Lorelli was learning that one of the most difficult aspects of friendship was being expected to fill the air with endless conversation. She struggled to find things to talk about, but Felicia was never short of something to say. When Felicia went to brush her teeth and wash her face, Lorelli sat on a bed. She was enjoying the silence until it dawned on her that Felicia had been a long time in the bathroom. She went out to investigate.

The door to the Gruoch Suite was solid oak and completely soundproof, so it wasn't until Lorelli opened it that she heard the yelling.

'Lori-chicken! Help! Someone . . . ! Anyone . . . !'

Lorelli tried the bathroom door handle. It was locked on the inside. She heard the hiss of rushing water and Felicia's fists against the wood as she pounded the door.

'Felicia, what's wrong?' asked Lorelli.

'The door won't open. Help . . . Lori-chicken! I'm too young and pretty to die!'

'What are you talking about?'

'I turned on the taps. I have to exfoliate otherwise my skin gets all blotchy. But they won't turn off again. The tap came off in my hand, then the door handle did the same. It's filling up with water. I'm going to drown!'

'Try not to panic,' said Lorelli. 'There will be overflow drainage.'

'It's blocked. Everything is blocked. The water is up to my waist and it's rising fast . . .'

'Ovid,' muttered Lorelli. She had no idea what he was up to, how he'd set up the trap or why, but she could spot his handiwork a mile off.

'Hold on.' Lorelli picked up a large porcelain pot with a blue printed design around the side. It was probably very old and very expensive but she had no choice. She tipped out the plant and yelled, 'Stand back!' She threw the plant pot at the door. It smashed into pieces but the door remained unbroken.

'You realise that was one of a pair.' Ovid was standing behind her holding a wrench, with a rope tied around his waist.

'What are you doing?' asked Lorelli.

'Rescuing your friend.' He leaned the wrench against the door, then tied the loose end of rope to the top of the banister. 'Now, my darling sister, if you value your life I suggest you step back into the bedroom.'

'Why?' asked Lorelli.

'Because when I make a hole in that bathroom door several gallons of water are going to gush out, dragging everything on this landing down the stairs unless it is tied securely.'

'What about you?'

'What do you think this is for?' He tugged the rope around his waist.

'What's happening?' yelled Felicia from the bathroom, frantic with fear.

'Felicia, this is Ovid. Listen very carefully. Get back and grab onto something.' Ovid turned to Lorelli. 'Obviously you are welcome to stay and get your neck broken as you are thrown down the stairs.' Ovid raised the wrench above his head.

Lorelli ducked back into the suite and closed the door, so she was unable to hear Ovid repeat his command to Felicia or the noise of the wrench smacking against the door three times. She could not hear the door break or the water gush out. When Lorelli stepped out, the wave had passed. Ovid was clinging onto the top banister, while Felicia was lying down on the cold, wet bathroom tiles.

'I . . . I thought I was going to die,' she said. 'I saw my whole life flash in front of my eyes.'

'That must have been simply wonderful,' said Ovid. He stepped into the bathroom and used the wrench on the tap to stop the flowing water. He offered Felicia his hand. 'You'd better get up.'

Felicia's hair was flattened against her face. She looked up at Ovid and wiped the drips from her face, smudging her make-up. 'You . . . You saved my life,' she sighed.

ACT II

Two Stories

Tom Paine found Dragos standing on the croquet lawn looking up at Thornthwaite Manor. The builder's rough palms were pressed together as though in silent prayer. Old Tom carried a gardening spade. Neither man looked concerned about the rain, the cold or the early hour.

'Morning, Dragos,' said Tom.

'Mister Tom. See how the old lady weeps?' Dragos indicated where the rain water gushed from one of the corners of the tower.

'Looks like the guttering needs clearing to me,' said Tom.

'We see different things.'

Old Tom nodded. 'What are your plans today?'

'Today I work on the southwest tower.'

'The bathroom by the Gruoch Suite needs looking at. Nurse Griddle tells me there was a problem with it.'

'The tower is the crutch that keeps the old lady on her feet.'

'Someone almost died in the bathroom.'

'Died?' Dragos turned to face the old gardener. 'Then I will take a look at it. Safety comes first.'

'Aye,' said Tom, 'and yet this old house has a long history of things not being safe. We're all hoping that's done with now.'

'It is my hope too,' said Dragos.

Old Tom poked a molehill down with his spade. 'I once knew a chap who used to talk to his marrows,' he said.

'What is this, marrow?'

'A big courgette.'

'I see.'

'Me and this fellow used to compete in the village fête. When it came to the biggest vegetable competition, no one else had a look-in.'

'You English have strange competitions.'

Tom nodded. 'Only I could never beat his marrows. Every single time, he won. When I asked how, he claimed it was because he talked to them.'

Dragos smiled at the idea. 'This is a funny story.'

'That's not the end. You see, I believed him and I really wanted to win, so I started talking to mine.'

Dragos raised an eyebrow. 'Did it help?'

'Not in the slightest.'

'Maybe you were not saying the right things,' suggested Dragos.

'Actually, as it turned out, this fellow was using illegal fertiliser. He bragged about it down the pub one night. That was why his marrows grew bigger. He lost his trophies and got a lifelong ban from vegetable competitions.'

Dragos laughed. 'I like this story. The meaning of it is that cheats do not prosper, yes?'

'I suppose, but also, mind who you tell your secrets to,' said Tom.

'I have a story as well. Mine is about my father. When I was a child, after my mother had gone, we lived in a small . . . what is the word?' Dragos mimed a roof over his head.

'A house?' suggested Tom.

'Like a house but less nice.'

'A hovel?'

'Yes, a hovel. We lived in this small hovel full of holes and filth and rats. Every night the wind would rattle through those holes. This was where I learned that buildings have feelings. If you listen carefully, you can hear what is wrong with them. My father was not a well man. He would sit in his old chair, a blanket over his twig legs, calling out, *Dragos, Dragos, I'm cold!* I wanted to help, so I found what I could to block the holes. First, I used newspaper. But the next night again he called, *Dragos, Dragos, I am still cold!* So I found some wood from the forest and blocked it with that, but the wind still rattled and the cold still came. *Dragos, Dragos, this cold will be the death of me.* This time I found a building site where men worked. I saw how they laid bricks and used mortar to hold them in place. When they stopped for lunch I went onto site and took some bricks and mortar. I carried them back and bricked up the holes. There were no more draughts.'

'Your father must have been pleased.'

'No. My father had died of hypothermia. I was too late. I could not save him, but I could save the building. By the time I had finished, that hovel was not a hovel. It was a house. It is a shame my father never lived to see it.'

'And the meaning of your story?' asked Tom.

Dragos shrugged. 'Dead men don't need houses.'

'Stories are all very well,' said Tom wistfully, 'so long as you don't go telling the wrong people the wrong kind of stories.'

'I am not here to rock boats.'

'I hope not,' said Tom. 'Remember, I vouched for you.'

'I am grateful.'

'So, the bathroom?' said Tom.

'I will take a look. Above all, we must protect this old lady.'

'And her children,' said Tom.

'And her children,' agreed Dragos.

A Splendid Breakfast

Lorelli had never seen a breakfast spread like it. There were plates of eggs, bacon, sausages, French toast, a selection of bread rolls and freshly squeezed orange juice. Lorelli stared at it all while Felicia made excitable chirruping noises and fragmented exclamations such as 'Gosh I . . .', 'What a . . .' and 'How very . . .'

Lorelli was surprised by Felicia's buoyant mood. She expected her to be plagued by nightmares reliving her near-death experience, but Felicia had stirred only once in her sleep. She had moaned something that sounded worryingly like Ovid's name before sighing and rolling over. Lorelli had barely slept a wink as she ran over the events in her head. The more she mulled it over, the more she knew Ovid had something to do with the bathroom death trap. It wasn't just the immaculate simplicity of the design. There was also a certain neatness about death by drowning following the fire in her room. Water and fire. But if Ovid was really back to his old ways, why did he save Felicia? What game was he playing?

'Oh, what a marvellous spread, Lori-chicken.' Felicia helped herself to a plateful of food.

'We don't usually eat like this,' said Lorelli.

'Now, Lori-chicken, I know you worry that people will think of you as spoilt and privileged, but remember, I'm your friend,' said Felicia. 'I like it.'

Hazel entered and placed a plate of light pastries on the table.

'Thank you, Hazel,' said Lorelli. 'But please do tell Beaufort that this is enough. I don't even think Ovid will be joining us.'

'Really? That is a shame,' said Felicia. 'I did so want to thank him for his brave rescue.'

'Rescue, miss?' said Hazel.

'It was just a stiff door and a plumbing problem in one of the bathrooms in the west wing,' said Lorelli.

'I could have died,' said Felicia. 'Lori-chicken tried to break down the door but she was too weak. Thankfully, Ovid arrived and saved my life.'

'I see, miss.' Hazel picked up a jug and topped up Felicia's glass with orange juice, but it was fuller than she expected and she slurped a little over the side, staining the tablecloth.

'You clumsy girl,' said Felicia.

'Felicia,' said Lorelli. 'Please don't speak to Hazel like that.'

'No, it was my fault,' said Hazel. 'I'm sorry.'

She wiped up the stain and ran out in such a hurry that she didn't notice she was still holding the jug or that Uncle Harry was coming the other way. Orange juice splashed onto his pale suit and blue shirt.

'I'm so sorry,' said Hazel.

'It's fine,' replied Uncle Harry calmly. 'It's only a suit.' He let her pass and poured himself a coffee. 'This all looks rather nice. We had better pass on our compliments to the chef. He gets very annoyed when we don't.'

He filled his plate and sat down at the table. 'I hear there was some excitement in the bathroom last night.'

'It was just a silly accident,' said Lorelli.

'Of course.' He stirred in a teaspoon of sugar and tasted the coffee. 'But it concerns me. First the chandelier, then the fire, now this. There are so many dangers in this old place. Having finally found you, I'd hate to lose you again.'

'Thornthwaite Manor is our home,' said Lorelli.

'Such a beautiful home,' said Felicia.

Uncle Harry picked up a plate and loaded on a selection of food. 'I know, but you have options.'

'What options?' asked Lorelli.

'You and Ovid could move in with me,' he said. 'I've got houses all over. I could buy another one around here if you wanted to keep on at the same school.'

'What do you mean, another one?' said Lorelli.

'I completed on the purchase of a property for Beaufort's restaurant in Little Fledgling this morning.'

'Oh, a restaurant in the village!' squealed Felicia. 'How wonderful.'

'Yes, it was quite a bargain too,' said Uncle Harry. 'I often find you can get a good price out of councils selling off unwanted property.'

'What property?' asked Lorelli suspiciously.

'It was the library,' said Uncle Harry.

'You're responsible for the library shutting?' said Lorelli. 'You can't. It's not right. You're putting Miss Wilde out of a job. Taking a library out of a village you might as well rip out its heart. It's . . .' She tried to remember all the things Miss Wilde had said about the importance of libraries but she was too angry. 'It's important and you're killing it,' she said.

'Now steady on,' said Uncle Harry. 'It's the council that is selling it. They're the ones who have removed the funding. I'm just buying a property that is for sale.'

'If you really want to be an uncle to us, then you will keep it open.'

'Keep it open? Lorelli, I'm a businessman. There is no monetary value in libraries.'

'I don't care about monetary value,' said Lorelli.

Uncle Harry glowered at her. Lorelli did not flinch. She had felt helpless when Miss Wilde told her about the library closing down, but if Uncle Harry was buying it then she could make a difference after all. She could save the library. She was prepared to argue all day if necessary. She would never give up. Perhaps Uncle Harry could see that, because he nodded and said, 'Oh, all right.'

'All right what?' said Lorelli.

'All right, I'll keep it open as a library.'

'You will?' said Lorelli.

'Yes.' Uncle Harry took her hand. 'For you.'

'I don't know what to say,' said Lorelli.

'You don't need to say anything,' said Uncle Harry. 'Properties, profit, money . . . These things have no value to me any more. Family is my priority now.'

Ovid's Bicycle

Prior to his cycle ride to Little Fledgling, Ovid ran the usual checks on his bike. Previous experience made it essential to test the brakes, ensure the inner tubes were clear and the saddle was secure. Looking for all possible signs of sabotage was an old habit that was difficult to break. He had just finished running a Geiger counter over the handlebars when Dragos stepped into the workshop.

'This is nice bicycle,' he said. 'Tom tells me you repaired it yourself.'

'Yes. It was little more than a frame when I found it,' replied Ovid.

Dragos inspected the bicycle. 'You have many skills,' he said.

'Thank you.' Ovid placed the Geiger counter on the table and picked up a handheld gas detector.

'Tom asked me to look at the bathroom.'

Ovid switched on the device and checked it for any unusually high readings. 'Which bathroom?'

'The one in the west wing.'

'Oh, that one. So is it all fixed now?'

'It was fixed before,' said Dragos seriously. 'Now it is safe.'

'What does that mean?'

'This bathroom trap was no accident. It was designed to do this by someone with many skills.'

Ovid switched off the gas detector and stood up to address Dragos. 'Have you told my sister this yet?'

'No. I came to see you first.'

'Then please do not tell her.'

'You would have me lie?'

'If you tell her it was a trap she will only worry,' said Ovid casually.

'Worry is no bad thing if it keeps people from danger.'

'My sister and I used to play tricks on each other—'

'Dangerous tricks,' interrupted Dragos.

'Yes, but that is over. I promise you.'

'So this bathroom was not one of your tricks?'

'Dragos, this really is none of your business. You have been employed to restore the house. You're a builder. That is all.'

'Yes, and now I must restore this bathroom. I do not want to find any more booby traps.'

'You are an employee,' stated Ovid. 'You are not a member of our family.'

Dragos nodded, unable or unwilling to meet Ovid's gaze before responding. 'I work for the old lady. She knows that family should be kind to family.'

Ovid replied quietly but firmly. 'Unless you want this situation to get worse, you must not tell Lorelli about it. If you tell her I did this, then she will start getting suspicious of me and then I'll get suspicious of her and, before we know it, we'll be back to how we used to be.'

'When you used to play dangerous tricks on each other.'

'Exactly.'

'You must promise, no more of this.'

'Cross my heart and hope to die.'

'Hope not to die is better,' said Dragos.

'It's an expression. It means . . . it just means I promise.'

'I will trust you, but be warned, you have made promise. To break it would be a betrayal of my trust.' Dragos thumped his chest with his fist.

Riding Pride

Tom Paine led the horses from the stables, saddled and ready to ride, but Lorelli still made a point of checking the buckles and reins for signs of tampering. Things were feeling too much like they used to feel. Lorelli had even found herself thinking about all those plots of her own that she had never got round to executing. She pushed these thoughts to the back of her mind. The last thing she wanted was to scare off Felicia. Normal people did not plot to kill each other.

Lorelli was dressed in her jet-black riding gear, while Felicia was sporting a pair of blood-red jodhpurs and an immaculate riding jacket.

'I take it you'll be riding Joy, Miss Lorelli.' Tom handed a sugar lump to the piebald mare.

'I will,' said Lorelli. 'Felicia will be on Pride. She's easier to control.'

'Aye. With Miss Lorelli on Joy, Pride will follow placidly enough,' Tom said, patting the chocolate-brown gelding.

'Oh, riding with my Lori-chicken on such a glorious day,' said Felicia. 'It's such a dream come true.'

'Actually, looks to me like rain's heading over,' said Tom.

'We don't mind getting wet, do we, Lori-chicken?'

'It's not you I'm worried about,' said Tom. 'Joy can get a little skittish in a storm.'

'Do you think it will be that bad?' asked Lorelli.

'I'm no weatherman,' replied Tom, 'but it's best to be prepared. As I recall, it was a clap of thunder that caused her to throw Master Ovid all those years ago.'

'Does Ovid ride too?' asked Felicia.

'Not since the fall,' said Lorelli.

'He blames the horse,' said Tom, 'but truth is, the master is always the one to blame. It's him giving the orders. The horse just does what he's told.'

'That's not entirely fair,' said Lorelli. 'A horse like Joy is always going to be a little unpredictable.'

'A good rider, like yourself, knows how much slack a horse can be given,' said Tom.

'You should not argue with your superiors,' said Felicia. 'These are Lori-chicken's horses. Everything here belongs to her. You're only a gardener.'

'And a day don't go by that I'm not grateful for that,' said Tom. 'But this estate is under our guardianship till the young masters come of age.'

'So you're a caretaker as well as a gardener,' said Felicia. 'Big fat deal.'

'Felicia, please don't be so rude,' said Lorelli, a little taken aback.

'Surely the whole point of serving staff is that you can treat them however you want,' she replied.

'That's not how it is here,' said Lorelli. 'Our staff are . . . well, they're more like family to us.'

'Yes, but family who can't answer back because you pay them.'

'It's not like that . . .' protested Lorelli.

'It makes no matter to me,' said Tom. 'Enjoy yourselves out there.' He handed the reins to Lorelli.

'Thank you, Tom,' she said.

Tom went into the stable and Lorelli helped Felicia onto Pride's back before lifting herself up into Joy's saddle.

'It is a shame Millicent couldn't have joined us,' said Lorelli.

'We haven't enough horses for her,' said Felicia. 'Besides, her father won't let her leave that horrible smelly butcher's. Since her mother disappeared, her dad has been really intense. He's probably worried that she'll run off too.'

'Do you know why she left?' Lorelli turned Joy off the path, across the lawn towards Orwell Hill. Pride followed. 'Father Whelan made a terrible accusation yesterday.'

'You mean that Mr Hartwell killed his wife, then chopped her up and sold her as prime cuts of meat?' said Felicia. 'Yes, he's been saying that to anyone who will listen.'

'It's not true, is it?' said Lorelli.

'Of course not,' said Felicia. 'Father Whelan is as mad as a barrel of cheese.'

'Yes, but you can't just go around accusing people of stuff like that. Why doesn't Mr Hartwell tell the police about Whelan and make him stop?'

'I don't know. Probably doesn't want to cause a fuss. No one listens to that mad priest.'

Lorelli dropped the reins a little and gave Joy a little tap with her heel so that she sped up. Father Whelan's wild accusations were by no means reliable, but there was, in her experience, often some truth in them.

Lorelli and Felicia had ridden halfway up the hill when they felt large droplets land on their heads. It wasn't long before the rain was bouncing off their riding hats and the view was lost in a thick cloud of drizzle.

'Maybe we should head back,' said Lorelli.

'I'm sure it's just a passing –' Pride lost his footing, producing a small terrified squeal from Felicia.

'We'll take shelter just over the next ridge,' said Lorelli. 'There's a hut by the old mine.'

'A mine. How divine. I say, that rhymes!' She giggled. 'What kind of mine is it, Lori-chicken?'

'It was supposed to be a gold mine.'

'Gold!' cried Felicia. 'How wonderful.'

'It's not wonderful. Our grandfather, Lord Silas, was a greedy man. Somehow he got it into his head that there was gold under the estate, but none was ever found. Only gas.'

The rickety hut and winch tower stood in a clearing. With its rotten wooden beams and broken roof it wasn't exactly cosy, but it did offer welcome shelter from the storm. Lorelli dismounted and tethered Joy to one of the posts, then helped Felicia off Pride.

'A gold mine. How adorably romantic,' said Felicia, following her under cover.

'My grandfather's first wife died down there. So did my grandfather when he threw himself in.' Lorelli peered into the lift. 'It's not romantic.'

'Oh, but death can be very romantic. You know, like in *Romeo and Juliet*, *Antony and Cleopatra*. In the old days, people were always dying romantically.' Felicia took off her riding hat and ran her fingers through her hair. 'So, what do you say? Shall we go down?' she asked.

'I'd rather not.'

'I'll bet it's really spooky down there. Go on, let's see.'

'As I say, I'm not that keen on—'

'Lori-chicken, I hope you're not telling me that you are scared of a silly old thing like the dark.'

Lorelli knew it was ridiculous to harbour any irrational fears when she had grown up with so many real threats, but it was true. She had been scared of the dark since the time she was trapped in a cupboard with a pipe feeding poisonous gas inside. Lorelli had blocked it up with her stockings, but what Ovid had not known was that she had been using the same cupboard to store a deadly snake. Thirty-seven minutes in a confined space with a deadly snake had been enough to give Lorelli a lasting fear of the dark.

'I do hope Lori-chicken isn't a bit of a chicken,' Felicia tittered. 'Oh, I'm sorry. I don't mean to be a meany. We don't have to go down there.'

'I'm not a chicken,' said Lorelli.

'No, I know. I was only teasing.'

'I'm not scared of the dark. And I'll prove it. Yes, let's go down.'

Memorial Picture House

Ovid chained his bike to a railing outside Little Fledgling Memorial Hall, then read the black-and-white poster on the noticeboard outside:

THE HEXFORD FILM SOCIETY
Proudly Presents:
The Hexford Cinema Season

A comprehensive history of cinema filmed in and
around the Hexford area.
Films shown every day this week at 11 a.m.
Please see the President of the Society, Dean
Griffiths, for further information.

Ovid pushed the heavy wooden door and stepped into the echoey atrium. A young man stood behind a counter. His hair was combed into a middle parting and he wore a T-shirt of an old horror film poster, oddly distorted by his portly belly.

'Could I have two tickets for today's film?' said Ovid.

'Really?' replied the man. 'Do you know what it is?'

'No.'

'Are you a member of the society?'

'Do I have to be?'

'No, but tickets are half price for members.'

'How much is it to join?'

'It's free . . . Actually, no, it's fifty pounds. That sounds like a lot, doesn't it? Twenty pounds? How about twenty-five pounds and you get a free pencil?'

'I think I'll just take the tickets,' said Ovid.

'Are you sure? We have a lot of fun. I'm Dean, the president.' He puffed out his chest and held up a leaflet. 'We meet here once a week and discuss films.'

'I'm afraid I don't know anything about films, so I'd only spoil it for the others.' Ovid was eager to extract himself from the conversation.

'At the present time we have a shortage of members in the society. None except yours truly.'

'So you meet with yourself once a week and discuss films.'

'That is correct.'

'I'll pay full price for the tickets, thank you. What's the film about?'

Dean opened a pamphlet and read from it. '*Hotel Nowhere* is a self-indulgent, sloppily directed and ill-conceived film, quite rightly panned by critics and ignored by audiences when it first came out. Now, finally, the Hexford Film Society is proud to give it the screening it so richly deserves.' He grinned. 'I wrote that.'

'It doesn't sound very good.'

'The review or the film?'

'The film.'

'Oh, no, it's terrible.'

'So why are you showing it?'

'It turns out there aren't actually that many films made in Hexford. So, two tickets, was it?' He pulled out two rolls of raffle tickets, one pink, one yellow. 'Standard or deluxe?'

'What's the difference?'

'A pound.'

'I mean, what's the difference in what you get?'

'You get a cushion with the deluxe.'

'Two deluxe tickets, please.'

Dean Griffiths tore off two yellow tickets. He was handing them to Ovid when Millicent stepped into the atrium. She shook her umbrella. 'I'm sorry I'm late,' she said.

'I've got the tickets.' Ovid held them up to show her, but Dean snatched them from his hand and tore them in half.

'Enjoy the film,' he said.

Keen to get away from the odd man, Ovid led Millicent into the empty hall.

'What are we watching?' asked Millicent.

'It's called *Hotel Nowhere*. Where do you want to sit?'

Millicent looked at the rows of vacant seats. 'I don't mind.'

Ovid chose a seat in the middle of a middle row. They sat down and Millicent handed him a cold plastic bag with something inside.

'What is it?'

'Meat.'

'Why did you bring a bag of meat?' asked Ovid.

'It's for your uncle. He ordered it yesterday. It's gazelle meat.'

'Right. Thanks.' Ovid placed the package under his chair. He had a strong suspicion that most dates did not involve a bag of smelly meat, but since this was his first, he couldn't be entirely sure.

Beaufort's Secret

Hazel was returning with a handful of fresh mint from the garden when she heard voices from inside the kitchen. She stopped to listen.

'I'm afraid there's been a delay.'

It was Uncle Harry's voice.

'Delay?' replied Beaufort. 'What delay?'

'Our project will have to be postponed.'

'Postponed?' proclaimed Beaufort. 'No. It cannot be postponed.'

'Don't worry. The restaurant will still go ahead.'

'Restaurant?' Beaufort spat the word. 'This is no mere restaurant. We are creating a shrine to the genius that is my food.'

'I knew you'd be like this,' said Harry.

Hazel could see the shadows of the two men. Beaufort was brandishing a large knife. Uncle Harry was keeping his distance.

'People will gather at this shrine as they once gathered around a manger in a Bethlehem stable.'

'I'm sorry. Are you comparing yourself to Jesus?' said Uncle Harry, clearly amused by the idea.

'Not myself. It is my food that is divine. This will be an experience like no other.'

'Yes, but there will be waiters and cooks and food . . . and hopefully big fat bills at the end,' said Uncle Harry with a chuckle. 'Besides, it will only be postponed for a short time.'

'I will tolerate no delay.'

'It's unavoidable, I'm afraid, but if you want to put your impatience to good use, you could help move things along.'

'What do you want?'

'A story,' said Uncle Harry.

'On what subject?'

'Isolation. A life of fear, loneliness, paranoia and an inescapable fate.'

'A tragedy then,' said Beaufort.

'No. There is hope in this story. There is a way out. But the message must be clear. The only way to escape fear is to start afresh. Our heroes must find a way out of their prison.'

'I see. It is a complex message you wish me to convey.'

'Yes, but can you do it?'

There was a long pause before Beaufort finally spoke.

'If I create this narrative, you will remove the obstacles that delay our project?'

'Exactly.'

'Then vacate my kitchen at once. I must prepare.'

Uncle Harry's shadow grew larger. He was walking towards the door. Hazel ducked behind the door in time to avoid being seen. He paused in the doorway. Hazel could see his face as he turned back and smiled at Beaufort.

'I look forward to tonight's meal.'

'Yes, you should,' said the chef. 'It will be *magnifique*.'

Silas's Mine

The only time Lorelli had ever ventured down the mine she had been ten years old. Things had been especially tense between her and Ovid at the time. It had been early November and Ovid had messed with Old Tom's fireworks so that they fired directly at her. Bent on revenge, Lorelli had looked into the possibility of laying a trap and luring Ovid down the mine, before plumping for the simpler idea of a game of French cricket and an exploding bat.

The lift had been bad enough back then. It was worse now. Lorelli glanced at Felicia as the rickety cage rattled its way down the shaft.

'To think we might find a nugget of gold and then I'd be as rich as you.' Felicia giggled. 'Imagine that. If I was just like you. Can you imagine it?'

The shifting circle of soft yellow light from the gas lantern lit up Felicia's eyes, causing Lorelli to wonder if there could be more to Felicia than met the eye. After all, the statue had been her idea. She had been the one who moved it to the east windowsill. The lamp swung away and threw her face into darkness. Had this whole riding expedition been a trap to lure Lorelli down this mine?

'If I was as rich as you, I'd go riding every day and we would have such marvellous adventures,' chirruped Felicia.

No, thought Lorelli. Felicia was a lot of things – annoying, silly, ridiculous – but she was no killer.

'There isn't any gold down here,' said Lorelli.

'I know, but it's fun to pretend. I love pretending things. I'm always imagining how things would be if I were rich.'

The lift shuddered and the mechanism creaked as they hit the bottom. Felicia stumbled. Lorelli grabbed her hand to keep her from falling.

'Here we are then,' said Lorelli. 'There's really not much else to see.'

'We can go back up if you're scared, Lori-chicken,' said Felicia.

'I am not scared,' replied Lorelli.

'Then why are you gripping my hand so tightly?'

Lorelli released her hand. She turned the lamp up to full beam, but it still only nibbled pathetically at the endless supply of darkness on the other side of the cage door.

'There's nothing down here,' said Lorelli.

Felicia opened the grate and stepped into the tunnel. She felt the damp wooden beams and craggy rock walls. Lorelli swung the lantern to highlight a row of pick axes. A pile of buckets threw strange shadows at the walls.

'How far does it go?' asked Felicia.

'I don't know.'

'Let's find out.'

Felicia bowed her head as she took a few more steps along the tunnel. Lorelli was desperately trying to think of a reason not to follow when she heard a low growl.

'What was that?' Felicia said.

For a moment they both listened. The second growl was louder than the first.

'It sounds like a good reason to leave,' said Lorelli. She turned to go but Felicia gripped her hands and held up the lantern. The *good reason to leave* stepped into the dim light. It had a large muscular body covered in spotted fur, whiskers and two green eyes that stared unblinkingly at Felicia.

'Lo— Lori-chicken?' Fear crept into Felicia's voice.

'Don't panic. Just make your way back to the lift, but slowly. No sudden movements.'

'Why . . . What is it?'

The *good reason to leave* showed its teeth and growled.

'It's a leopard,' said Lorelli. 'No sudden—'

'A leopard!' Felicia screamed. Lorelli jumped back into the lift. She dragged Felicia behind her. As her arm swung, the lantern went out. The leopard roared and jumped. Lorelli slammed the gate shut and scrambled to find the control. The leopard crashed into the metal gate. Lorelli's finger found the UP button. Felicia whimpered. Lorelli pressed the control so hard her finger hurt.

'Lori-chicken,' whispered Felicia, 'why is there a leopard in your mine?'

'That is a very good question,' said Lorelli.

Hotel Nowhere

The non-fiction books in Thornthwaite Manor had yielded disappointing results on the subject of dates, so Ovid had been forced to delve into the less familiar fiction section. His research provided him with several accounts of dates, which he had studied for common themes and repeating patterns. After writing up his results he had concluded that a successful date required at least two of the following:

- Eye contact
- Laughter
- Physical contact (specifically hand holding and/or kissing)

The first two requirements posed no problems to Ovid. Any fool could look at someone and laugh. It was the third factor that concerned him. His palms were sweaty at the best of times. Sitting next to Millicent in Little Fledgling Memorial Hall, they were so damp he had soaked his trousers trying to dry them. Kissing wasn't even a consideration.

The film provided a welcome distraction. Dramatic orchestral music played over the opening titles, and a boy walked down a long train corridor with the cold English landscape whizzing past outside. Eventually the boy reached a cabin where there were two more children.

The music faded away as the train pulled into the station and the three children prattled on in squeaky American accents. Outside the station, a sign read 'Welcome to nowhere', but Ovid recognised it as Little Fledgling train station.

'That's here,' whispered Millicent.

The children came out of the station, still yabbering on in annoying voices, then bumped into a man holding a bent umbrella and wearing a bent top hat.

'Say, mister,' said one of the children, 'where the flaming jelly bean are we anyway?'

'Nowhere,' replied the man in a plummy English voice. 'I am here to take you to Hotel Nowhere. There's nowhere in the world like Hotel Nowhere.'

Ovid looked at Millicent but she was staring at the screen, open-mouthed. It was showing Thornthwaite Manor. Lightning snaked across the image and thunder rumbled.

'Welcome to Hotel Nowhere,' said the strange man.

'Gee, it looks kinda spooky,' said one of the children.

Millicent leaned over and whispered, 'It's your house.'

Ovid was alarmed by the closeness of her lips, but he was unable to tear his eyes away from the screen. With its faded curtains, brown furniture and oil paintings, Thornthwaite Manor was exactly as it had been before the great fire.

In the film, the annoying American kids had been sent on holiday to a weird English hotel where strange things kept happening. The children's response to most of these situations was to scream and run around a lot. It was a terrible film, with only two points of interest for Ovid. The first was a brief glimpse of a boy's face in an upstairs window of Thornthwaite Manor. It was only a fleeting shot but it lingered long enough for Ovid to see the boy's green eyes. Nothing was filmed inside the manor, but there was a scene around the entrance to the old mine, in which grubby-faced miners could be seen working in the background. Ovid stopped listening to whatever the characters were going on about when he noticed that one of the miners bore more than a passing resemblance to Dragos.

When the film finally finished, following a crescendo of screaming and running, the bright hall lights came on, making Ovid blink. 'What did you think?' he asked.

'I liked seeing the bits filmed around here,' said Millicent. 'Was that your father in the window?'

'I suppose so. I've only ever seen old portraits of him, and they're all gone now.'

'It's hard to remember faces, isn't it?' said Millicent. 'It's only been a few weeks since Mum went and I already find it hard to remember hers.'

'Yes, but you'll see her again, won't you?'

'I don't know. Dad is still pretty upset with her.'

'What about you?'

Millicent's eyes clouded over for a moment. 'She didn't say goodbye to me either.'

'I'm sorry.'

'Don't be. Dad says we're well rid of her.' Millicent bent down and picked up the bag of meat. 'Don't forget your gazelle.'

Ovid's research had entirely failed to supply him with a reply to this statement, so he plumped for: 'Would you like to do something else now? We could go for a milkshake.'

'I promised my dad I'd come straight home after the film. He thinks I'm here with Felicia.'

'Felicia is still at ours,' said Ovid.

'At the manor?'

'Yes. She stayed last night.'

'You'll never get her out now.'

'She was almost stuck there permanently.' Ovid allowed himself a small, wicked smile.

'What do you mean?' Millicent asked.

'She got trapped in a bathroom. I had to smash the door down.'

'You saved her?'

Ovid couldn't tell if Millicent sounded impressed, shocked or horrified. The bitterness in her laughter didn't sound like the kind of laughter described in his date-research material. The fleeting glance of fear was not the eye contact he had imagined. She leaned forward so quickly he didn't have time to recoil. The kiss she planted on his cheek was brief. She had a cold nose. None of it was as he had imagined, but before he'd had time to analyse the data, Millicent had gone.

A History
of Murder

Nurse Griddle discovered Uncle Harry halfway up a ladder in the library of Thornthwaite Manor.

'Mr Marshall,' she said. 'May I help you?'

'It's remarkable. This whole place goes up in flames and a room filled with paper survives.'

'This library was constructed by Lord Willard in 1832. He treasured books above all else so kept them protected in a solid stone room with a nine-inch-thick door.'

'How fascinating.'

Nurse Griddle deflected his smile with a stern stare. 'Are you looking for anything in particular?'

'Lorelli mentioned a history of the family written by their late butler, Alfred Crutcher.'

'May I ask why you are interested in the history of a family you have shunned for so many years?'

'When my sister married Lord Thornthwaite she made me a part of the family too.'

'A part you have avoided playing for some time,' said Nurse Griddle.

'True.' Uncle Harry climbed down the ladder to address the nurse. 'It's never too late to make amends.'

'And so the long-lost uncle comes in search of . . . what exactly? Forgiveness? Redemption?'

'I want to put things right.'

'By giving money to a pair of children whose lives have been torn apart by greed?'

'My methods may be clumsy but my intention is honest.'

'These children deserve honesty.'

'So you are honest with them, are you?' He picked up a paper knife with an ornate snake-like handle. He tested its sharpness against his index finger. 'They didn't even know I existed.'

'It is our responsibility to protect them.'

'Yes. What protective guardians you are too. The twins' lawyer tells me that until they come of age this estate lies in your hands?'

'Those are the conditions of the will, yes.'

'I also understand that if they meet an unfortunate end the whole thing goes to the servants.'

'In that unlikely and undesirable eventuality, that is the case. There are no surviving heirs.'

'Then you would benefit greatly from their death.'

'Understand this, Mr Marshall: all my life I have tended Ovid and Lorelli's scratches and scrapes. I have bandaged their wounds, found antidotes for their poisons and extracted bullets. I have nursed them to good health and kept them safe. I will continue to do so as long as they need me.'

'It is to your credit,' admitted Uncle Harry. 'I'm sure Tom would say the same, albeit with some obscure gardening reference.'

'Is your intention to insult us all?' demanded Nurse Griddle.

'No, but while you see these twins as the continuation of a noble aristocratic family, I see a pair of my sister's kids who need an influence who isn't on the payroll and would gain nothing from their deaths.'

'Here at Thornthwaite Manor, we don't need to share blood to consider ourselves a family.'

'It isn't the blood shared that concerns me,' said Uncle Harry. 'It is the blood spilt.'

Nurse Griddle strode across the library and for a moment Uncle Harry thought she was about to walk out, but she reached up and plucked out a book. It was a brown hardback with no title or author name on the cover. She handed it to him. 'This is Alfred's history of the family. I hope you find what you are looking for.'

Uncle Harry opened it to the title page:

The Thornthwaite Legacy
Or
A History of Murder
By Alfred Crutcher

'*A History of Murder*,' he read out loud.

'Alfred did always have a tendency towards the melodramatic,' said Nurse Griddle.

'I can see that.' He flicked through its pages. 'May I borrow it?'

'It is not my place to stop you,' said Nurse Griddle, 'but regardless of what it says about their ancestors, Lorelli and Ovid deserve to be judged on their own merits. Theirs is a fresh page in this history.'

Half-truths and Lies

Ovid found his sister sitting alone in the drawing room, her chin resting on her hands as she considered the game of chess.

'Where's Felicia?' asked Ovid.

'Gone home.'

He sat down opposite her and placed the bone tortoise beside the chessboard. 'So,' he said, 'have you decided what to do next?'

'I'm considering the options.' Lorelli picked up the tortoise. 'I can see what Millicent means. There is a resemblance.'

'The shell?'

'The eyes.'

'We have the same eyes.'

Ovid took back the tortoise and Lorelli returned her attention to the game. After a couple of minutes of contemplative silence, she took Ovid's rook with her bishop, then balanced the piece on the tortoise's back. 'What are you up to?' she asked.

'It was your move,' said Ovid.

'You know what I mean.'

'No, I'm afraid you'll need to be clearer.' Ovid picked up the rook and put the tortoise back in his pocket.

'The bathroom was one of your traps,' said Lorelli.

Ovid shrugged. 'No one got hurt.'

He took her knight with his queen and handed her the piece.

Lorelli took it. 'Felicia is under the impression that you're her knight in shining armour.'

'That's funny.'

'Is that what this is, a big joke? What about the leopard? Is that a joke too?'

'I'm sorry? What?'

Lorelli searched his face for some indication that he was putting on an act, but she could not tell. He was a well-practised liar. 'The leopard down the mine,' she said. 'Or are you going to deny that one?'

'Silas's mine? I haven't been down there for years. How did a leopard get down there?'

'That's what I'm asking you.'

'You always assume I'm behind things.'

'You usually are.'

'Usually, yes,' admitted Ovid. 'But not this time. Maybe the leopard has something to do with Old Tom or Nurse Griddle, or . . .' His voice trailed away as he brought to mind the man in the film who looked like Dragos. 'Half-truths and lies,' he said. 'That's all we have.'

'Do you know what I think?' said Lorelli. 'I think you're trying to blame anyone but yourself.'

'That's because I'm not to blame,' protested Ovid.

'Aren't you?' Lorelli moved her queen forward, putting it in the firing line of Ovid's.

'Should I feel threatened?' he asked.

'If you do, then back down,' said Lorelli.

'Never.' Ovid took Lorelli's queen with his. Without a moment's consideration, she took his with her remaining knight.

'You could have moved away,' said Lorelli. 'We didn't have to exchange queens.'

'I prefer a level playing field.'

'I don't believe that for a second. So this leopard . . .'

Ovid placed his hand on his heart. 'My dear sister, I swear that I have no idea why there is a leopard down the – Gazelle!' he said, interrupting his own sentence as the thought struck him.

'What?' said his sister, understandably confused.

'I read a book on the hunting habits of wild animals once. I was looking for ideas and I remember reading that leopards eat gazelle.'

'So?'

'So I just picked up a batch of gazelle meat that Uncle Harry ordered.'

'Why would Uncle Harry put a leopard in the mine?'

'Why would anyone?' said Ovid. 'And yet, according to you, there is one there. Besides, do you trust him?'

'He's been nothing but good to us,' said Lorelli. 'He's putting us in his will, not the other way around.'

'It's too big a coincidence.'

'Why did you pick it up?'

131

'What?'

'You've been to the butcher's, have you?' Lorelli said with a goading wink at her brother.

Ovid blushed. 'No. Millicent gave it to me.'

'You took her on a date?' said Lorelli excitedly.

'It was not a date.' Ovid slammed his hand down on the table, knocking his king over.

'Are you resigning, dear brother?'

Ovid put his king back on its square and stood up. 'No. But that's enough game-playing for one evening.'

Adam Farthing

The only musical instrument in Thornthwaite Manor to survive the great fire was an eighteenth-century harpsichord. After leaving Lorelli in the drawing room, Ovid walked briskly to the music room, thinking it a good place to gather his thoughts. However, his pace slowed as he got closer and he heard its twangy notes playing a bright, cheerful tune.

He pushed the door open to find Uncle Harry and Mr Farthing standing next to the ornate keyboard, listening to Adam Farthing play.

'I'd be careful,' said Ovid. 'I seem to remember the piano blew up the last time you did that.'

Adam stopped playing. He looked up and Ovid instantly saw a difference in him. Gone was the brash, self-confident boy, leaving in his wake a far more timid creature. His fair hair was neatly combed. He avoided direct eye contact. He seemed uncomfortable in his own skin.

'Ovid,' said Uncle Harry. 'I understand you two know each other.'

'Yes,' replied Ovid. 'How are you, Adam?'

'I'm very –' He interrupted himself by tapping his

fingertips on his temple, then he said in a quieter voice, 'I'm making good progress, thank you.'

'Adam is seeing a new specialist,' said Mr Farthing.

'A specialist in what?' asked Ovid.

'Doctor Mingus is a behavioural correctologist,' said Mr Farthing. 'She specialises in people who are creative with the truth.'

'You mean liars,' said Ovid.

Adam tapped his head and blinked rapidly. 'We don't use that word,' he said quickly. 'I'm learning to distinguish the truth from what I want to be true. Doctor Mingus says . . .' Lorelli entered the room and Adam's words drifted away.

Ovid noticed the look on Adam's face. 'So?' he said. 'What is it you *want* to be true?'

'I . . .' Adam faltered.

'Adam?' said Lorelli. 'What brings you here?'

'He's here because of me,' said Mr Farthing.

'And you're here because of me,' said Uncle Harry. 'And since I'm the one paying, shall we get on with the business at hand?'

'Of course. I'm so sorry.' Mr Farthing opened his case and searched through it before remembering that he had already removed the document he was looking for. He handed it to Uncle Harry. 'It just needs your signature.'

Uncle Harry took a pen from his inside pocket.

'Lorelli, Ovid, I'd like you to witness this.'

'Actually, you'll need an independent person to do that,' said Mr Farthing.

'I'm sure you can jump through all the legal requirements for me, once this is done,' said Uncle Harry.

'Really the witness should be present at the point of signature,' blustered Mr Farthing.

'Charge me for the inconvenience,' said Uncle Harry firmly.

He handed the document to the twins. They read it together. It stated that, in the eventuality of his death, Harry Marshall's possessions and assets would be divided equally among them. They both read it twice, then handed it back to him. He took a fountain pen from his pocket and signed his name at the bottom.

'And so it is done,' said Uncle Harry. 'You are now the heirs to my estate.'

'Is that it?' said Ovid.

'That's it,' announced Uncle Harry. 'Bernard, perhaps you would join me for a celebratory drink. I feel like marking this occasion.'

'Well, I . . .'

'I'm afraid I'm not good at taking no for an answer. Never have been when celebrating is concerned. Or drinking for that matter.'

'I'd rather not leave my son unattended,' said Mr Farthing.

'Dad,' said Adam, 'I'll be fine.'

'Very well. A small one.'

'Lorelli, Ovid,' said Uncle Harry, 'I'll see you in the dining room shortly.'

The two men took their leave and Adam moved away from the harpsichord. Ovid lowered the lid. Adam stared at Lorelli, while she looked at anything except him.

No one spoke for an uncomfortably long time until Ovid broke the silence.

'Do you know what?' he said. 'I've just remembered something I need to do before dinner.'

Ovid left the room. Lorelli waited until she was sure he had gone before she spoke. 'Why did you come?' asked Lorelli.

'I wanted to see you,' replied Adam.

'I got your last letter.'

'Writing things down helps put my thoughts in order.'

'I'm not sure it does for me,' said Lorelli, thinking about her own failed attempts at writing.

'Doctor Mingus says everyone is different and that's okay,' said Adam. 'She says we can control our own lies, and if we do, it stops them growing bigger. Sometimes, in group, she gets us to draw honesty pies.'

'What does that mean?' asked Lorelli.

'You draw a big round pie, then imagine you're taking a bite out of it every time you tell a lie. Whatever is left is how truthful you are. My truth partner says the honesty pie is stupid, but I tell her that's the point. It makes you see how silly it is. It stops you being scared of the truth.'

Lorelli had no desire to think about the size of her honesty pie. She said, 'So your truth partner is a girl,' then instantly regretted it, realising how it sounded.

'Yes, but I don't want to talk about her,' said Adam. 'I want to talk about . . . I'm trying to be honest in what I say . . . and that means being honest about how I feel.' He fixed her with his gaze.

'Adam, I . . .' Lorelli took a small step back.

'I like you, Lorelli. I just want to know how you feel about me.'

Lorelli felt her body stiffen. She felt strangely aware of her nose. She tried to avoid Adam's gaze but it was unavoidable. She was struck by how much he had changed. His directness unnerved her. His intensity scared her. Her own feelings terrified her.

A Good Man

Ovid followed Uncle Harry and Mr Farthing to the boxing room. He took the upstairs entrance while the two men went through the door on the ground floor. Ovid snuck onto the balcony, then watched as Uncle Harry sat on the side of the boxing ring and poured two glasses of wine.

'That's enough, thank you.' Mr Farthing moved his glass away.

Ovid shifted to get a better view. A floorboard creaked under his foot. Mr Farthing looked up at the balcony. 'Who's up there?'

'Stop being so jumpy,' said Uncle Harry. 'There's no one up there. This old wreck is full of creaks. Never mind repairing it. It would be kinder to put it out of its misery.'

'I'm sorry.' Mr Farthing took a small, cautious sip of wine. 'You see, mine is not an entirely happy association with this old house.'

Uncle Harry gulped from his glass. 'Nor mine, but let's not dwell on the past.'

'I would have thought, given your situation, you would spend a great deal of time dwelling on the past.'

'You're wrong. The present is my concern. And the future.'

'When do you plan on telling them the truth?'

'In time.'

'Why not be honest from the start?'

'I'm concerned that if they do not see me as part of their future, they won't bother with me at all. So here's to the future, whatever it brings.' Uncle Harry clinked glasses and downed a mouthful of wine. 'Thank you, Bernard.'

'I have done very little.'

'Yes, but the twins know you, and that's important.'

'Knowing me isn't the same as trusting me.'

'Yours is the hand that drew up their parents' will. They called you when they wanted to make an alteration. Your involvement in this affair gives them consistency and reminds them that they are in charge of their own fates.'

'I suppose . . .'

'Ovid and Lorelli can escape their fate, but they must be led gently. It must come from them. The most persuasive voice is one's own. They must be their own liberators if they are to start a new chapter.'

Mr Farthing took the smallest of sips from his wine glass. 'I hope you can help them.'

'So do I. Now, I should get to the dining hall. Beaufort is cooking something special tonight.'

'Yes, I should get Adam out of here too. I shall send a copy of the new will to your team of lawyers.'

'Thank you, Bernard.' Uncle Harry gave his hand such a firm shake that wine splashed out of his glass.

'You're a good man, Harry Marshall,' said Mr Farthing.

'I'm trying to be,' replied Uncle Harry.

Incomplete Pictures

Ovid dashed along the corridor ahead of Uncle Harry and Mr Farthing, past numerous paintings, blackened and burnt by the great fire. It felt fitting to live in a house full of incomplete pictures. Nothing was ever clear in Thornthwaite Manor. Ovid was keen to discuss what he had overheard, but as he burst into the music room Lorelli and Adam both jumped back away from each other.

'Oh, sorry,' said Ovid. 'I didn't mean to interrupt anything.'

'You haven't. You didn't. What do you want?' asked Lorelli.

'There's something Uncle Harry hasn't told us.'

'Everyone's got something they haven't told us,' said Lorelli.

'Doctor Mingus says we all have to be selective with what we say,' said Adam. 'Even when we know the truth, we can never know the whole truth. In the end, all we can do is be honest with ourselves.'

Ovid tried to exchange a knowing glance with his sister, but she was gazing at Adam. 'How can we be honest with ourselves when no one has ever been honest with us?' she said.

'It is possible,' said Adam. 'But it isn't easy.'

Ovid was beginning to wonder if they had even noticed him. 'Farthing knows something that Harry hasn't told us. What is it?'

'I don't know,' said Adam.

'Something about him not being a part of our future.'

Adam tapped his head. 'I don't know.'

'Don't you?' said Ovid.

'No!' shouted Adam, tapping faster and harder on the side of his head.

'Because if you're lying to us again . . .'

'Leave him alone,' said Lorelli.

Ovid turned to look at her. Her cheeks were flushed.

The door opened and Uncle Harry and Mr Farthing returned. 'Everyone having fun?' asked Uncle Harry.

'Adam, it's time to go,' said Mr Farthing.

'Yes, Father,' said Adam timidly.

'And it's time we got to the dining room too,' said Uncle Harry. 'Beaufort is making something of a treat for us this evening.'

'Adam, you and your father would be most welcome to stay for dinner if you like,' said Lorelli.

'I . . . er . . .'

'No,' said Mr Farthing firmly. 'We have abused your hospitality quite enough for one day. We will take our leave.'

'Besides,' said Uncle Harry, 'I dread to think how Beaufort would respond to two more mouths to feed. He assures me this evening's meal is going to be something very special.'

'I'll show you out,' said Ovid.

'Goodbye, Adam,' said Lorelli. 'Thank you for visiting.'

'Goodbye, Lorelli. It's been . . . It was a . . .' He tapped his head. '. . . It was good to see you.'

Ovid led Adam and his father out of the room, and Uncle Harry turned to Lorelli. 'Interesting boy,' he said.

'I suppose,' said Lorelli, gathering herself. 'I don't really know him. Not all that well anyway. He visited with his father last year and . . .'

Uncle Harry placed a hand on her shoulder. 'I wasn't prying,' he said. 'You don't have to tell me anything you don't want to. I want to earn your trust, but you already have mine.'

Fish for Dinner

As far as Hazel was concerned, Beaufort had transformed the kitchen into an exotic kingdom filled with rich aromas and endless possibilities. The hiss and steam of the frying food were like dramatic stage effects in a magic show. Beaufort didn't make meals. He made miracles.

Beaufort's sporadic commentary rarely involved any specific explanations of what he was doing. Instead, it was mostly made up of obscure comments such as, 'If you cook with your entire body, your consumers will consume with theirs,' and, 'A cook must be as fit as an athlete, as precise as a scientist and as subtle as the devil.'

Hazel's main job was to ensure he was not interrupted, so she was alarmed to feel the soft brush of Cowell's fur against her leg. Beaufort was too busy frying fish to spot the cat. Hazel jumped off the stool and had nearly reached her tail when the door opened and Nurse Griddle stepped into the room. Beaufort threw a fish into the pan, sending clouds of steam into the atmosphere, obscuring the French cook from view. Cowell ran under a table.

Nurse Griddle coughed and exclaimed, 'What on earth is going on? I can't see a thing.'

'No sightseers,' said Beaufort. 'This is a crucial moment.'

'I am no sightseer!' cried Nurse Griddle.

A second fish went in, creating more thick steam.

From within the cloud, Beaufort cried out, '*Madame*, I do not know who you are, but now is not the time. 'Azel, do your duty.'

'*Oui*, chef.' Hazel was watching Cowell creeping towards the smell of frying fish.

'Hazel?' said Nurse Griddle. 'Are you in here too?'

'Yes, ma'am. It would probably be best if you left.'

'Why are you letting this man order you around?'

'If you please, ma'am,' said Hazel, 'Beaufort is an artist. He must not be distracted.'

'An artist? This place is hotter than the kitchens of hell. Messier too.'

'Would you judge Picasso by his studio?' said Beaufort. 'Would you tell Beethoven to tidy his room?'

'I'm sure both those gentlemen had very good housekeepers to tidy up after them,' replied Nurse Griddle.

'*Oui*. And I have 'azel, except you are currently distracting her. Now, please be so kind as to leave us.'

'I certainly shall. Hazel, we're leaving.'

'No.' The word came out of Hazel's mouth with such force that it caught her by surprise.

The hiss of another fish hitting the frying pan hid the gasp from Nurse Griddle. 'No? What do you mean, no?'

'I mean, no,' said Hazel.

'Quite aside from the fact that I have a superior position in the house, I am your mother.'

'Mrs Bagshaw is my mother. You gave me away.' Hazel was unable to contain herself. She didn't care about Nurse Griddle's feelings. She only cared about Beaufort.

'This is neither the time nor the place for this discussion,' exclaimed Nurse Griddle.

'I'm staying,' said Hazel firmly.

With all the smoke, Hazel couldn't see Nurse Griddle, but she could tell she was angry. 'You had better think long and hard about the decisions you make.'

'I have. This is what I want,' said Hazel.

'You have made that very clear now.' Nurse Griddle slammed the door on the way out. Hazel got back to the cat problem. Cowell was poised on her hind legs, preparing to jump up onto the counter.

'Beaufort – I mean, chef . . .' said Hazel.

Her warning was cut short by a large chopping knife flying across the kitchen and landing directly in front of the cat. Cowell let out a panicked screech and scarpered from the kitchen.

'You could have killed her!' exclaimed Hazel.

'Yes, my aim was a little off,' said Beaufort.

'She's a cat.'

''Azel, a kitchen is no place for a cat. Remember, we are the top of the food chain. If it can be killed, it can be eaten. Now, go gather tonight's audience for the performance. Tonight it is something new. Something dramatic. Tonight I will transport them to a brave new world.'

Bring on the Darkness

Ovid, Lorelli and Uncle Harry sat down at the dining table. Three places were set but the food was yet to arrive. Uncle Harry sipped his wine and leant back in his chair. 'I have to say, it feels as though a weight has been lifted off my shoulders. All these years I've been gathering this fortune with no sense of purpose. I can die happy now that I know it's going to my family.'

'And when you do die happy we get the lot, do we?' said Ovid.

Uncle Harry chuckled. 'I do hope that you're not thinking about bumping me off for my money.'

'And what if I was?' said Ovid. 'How would you suggest I did it? Poison your food? Or perhaps there's an easier way to knock you off.'

'Ovid,' scolded Lorelli.

'No, I'm interested,' said Ovid.

Uncle Harry allowed himself a smile. 'All right, I'll play this game. How would I kill me if I was you? Poisoning would certainly work, but I think I'd rather something a bit more dramatic. Perhaps you could tamper with the brakes in my car.'

'Or trap you down a mine with a wild animal,' said Ovid.

Uncle Harry stared back at Ovid, unsure what to say.

Lorelli turned to look at him too, but before he could reply Hazel entered carrying a tray with three small saucers. She placed them in front of Ovid, Lorelli and Uncle Harry. In the centre of each saucer was a small green globule on a silver spoon.

'What is this?' said Ovid.

'It's an amuse bouche,' said Beaufort, following Hazel into the room. 'It is a flavour to enliven your taste buds before a meal.'

Ovid leaned over to examine it. 'It looks like someone sneezed,' he said.

'Tonight's meal will be presented without the distraction of vision.'

'What?' said Lorelli.

'It will be eaten in the dark. Are you ready?'

'Absolutely,' said Uncle Harry. 'Bring on the darkness.'

Hazel switched off the light. Ovid picked up the spoon, sniffed it, then tasted its contents. As soon as it hit his taste buds it took his breath away. It was minty, sour and spicy. It was horrible. He heard Lorelli gasp and Uncle Harry cough.

'What was that?' asked Ovid.

Beaufort's voice spoke out of the darkness. 'Tonight I present a story told entirely through flavour. Some stories begin with a simple footstep, some begin with a bang. This palate cleanser is the scene-setting prologue that prepares you for the narrative of this meal.'

'The narrative of a meal?' said Ovid.

'Silence,' commanded Beaufort. 'Your taste buds are tingling. Your mouth is burning. The fire must be put out. Your next course awaits.'

Desperate to take away the flavour, Ovid found a bowl in front of him and lifted it to drink. It was ice cold, sweet, refreshing and delicious. He devoured it and was overcome by the sensation of having jumped out of a burning building into a cold river. It was as though the image was being projected through his mouth. He had never experienced anything like it.

He heard Lorelli sigh.

'Turn the next page,' said Beaufort.

This time Ovid's hand found a bread stick, but the texture and shape made him think of a wooden raft. In his mind's eye, he had climbed out of the water onto the raft. He lay down as it carried him downstream.

As the meal went on, Beaufort alerted them to each course and they continued to eat in silence. Ovid became further removed from his surroundings. He was immersed in the story. The raft travelled along the river, down fast-flowing rapids before the river calmed. He caught a fish and ate it raw. It was delicious, as though the river itself had seasoned and cooked it to perfection. The raft drifted to the side of the riverbank where he got off. He was alone in his story. He walked through a field of strawberries, crossed a moat and entered a grand old castle. He was thirsty. He grabbed a glass from a shelf and gulped it down. It tasted like lost memories. He went in search of someone but every room was empty. Fear entered his thoughts. How could such a large house feel so empty?

'Where is everyone?' said a voice. It was Lorelli. She must have been experiencing the same. Ovid reached out to take her hand but found an apple. He took a bite. It was the most delicious thing he had ever eaten. Tears sprang to his eyes. It tasted like freedom.

A thud on the table brought him back to reality.

'What was that?' he asked.

'Something's wrong,' said Lorelli.

'No interruptions,' said Beaufort.

'It's Mr Marshall,' said Hazel. 'He's collapsed.'

The lights came on suddenly and Ovid saw Uncle Harry lying face down in his food.

Business as Usual

When the ambulance arrived, the twins stood in the games room, watching from the window as its flashing blue lights disappeared up the driveway, carrying Uncle Harry to the hospital. It all felt like something out of a dream. Lorelli's thoughts were muddy and confused by Beaufort's narrative meal. Being drawn out of the story so suddenly had left her with an uncomfortable unresolved feeling. Whenever she closed her eyes, she could still picture the long corridors in the empty house. The nagging fear that something was wrong had not yet left her.

'What an eventful day it's turned out to be,' said Ovid.

Lorelli turned to her brother. 'I hardly think eventful is the right word,' she said. 'Harry is being rushed to hospital.'

'So? It's not my fault,' said Ovid.

'Uncle Harry collapses five minutes after you've brought up the idea of poisoning his food on the same night that he has put us in his will,' said Lorelli.

'What are you suggesting?'

'Just tell me the truth,' said Lorelli. 'Did you have anything to do with this?'

Ovid picked up a clock from the windowsill that had lost its hands in the fire. 'This has never worked,' he said. 'I don't know why we keep it.'

'Because it's always been here,' said Lorelli. 'Stop avoiding the question. I know the bathroom was you.'

'All right, it was one of my designs,' said Ovid, 'but that trap was three years old. I made it in retaliation for that time you bred those poisonous toads in the pond. I'd forgotten all about it.'

'I don't believe you.' Lorelli took the clock from Ovid and placed it back on the windowsill. 'I think you wanted to scare off Felicia because you can't stand me having friends.'

'Friends? You don't even like her.'

'I'm not trying to kill her though.'

'So you admit I'm right.'

'If you admit you tried to kill her.'

'Kill her?' exclaimed Ovid. 'I was the one who saved her life.'

Lorelli turned to leave. 'I don't know what you're up to, but I know you too well to believe anything you say.'

Hazel stepped into the room and began to clear the table.

'Hazel,' said Lorelli. 'Let me help.'

'There's no need, miss.' She quickly and efficiently stacked the dishes.

'What do you think, Hazel?' said Ovid.

'About what, sir?'

'Lorelli thinks I poisoned Uncle Harry. You've been in the kitchen all day. Have you seen me dropping anything suspicious into the food?'

'No. No one has been near the food except Beaufort, and he would never poison anyone.'

'How can you be so sure?' said Ovid.

'Because he wouldn't. If that's all . . .' Hazel took her leave.

'What is it about this house?' asked Lorelli. 'It's as though secrecy is built into the brickwork. Aren't you tired of it all?'

'Certainly I am,' said Ovid. 'Let's tell the truth. So, how long have you been writing to Adam?'

'I . . .'

'It's not so easy, is it?'

Lorelli met her brother's eyes, but they were as unreadable as they were impenetrable.

Moving the Story On

Old Tom said he would take the twins to visit Uncle Harry in the hospital the following afternoon, so in the morning they caught the bus to Little Fledgling. They barely spoke on the way, so there was no need for either of them to lie about where they were going. They parted ways at the bus stop and Lorelli walked straight to the library where she found Miss Wilde surrounded by boxes of books. The shelves were half empty, but Miss Wilde was sitting on the floor, hunched over a large book. When she looked up, it took a moment for her to blink herself out of the story she was reading.

'Lorelli,' she said. 'Sorry. I'm supposed to be clearing up this place but I keep getting distracted. Books are rather distracting, aren't they? I suppose that's their appeal.'

'You can stop packing,' said Lorelli. 'It's my uncle buying the library.'

'Your uncle?'

'Harry Marshall. He wanted to turn it into a restaurant but he's promised to keep it as a library.'

'Harry Marshall, the property magnate? What would he want with a library?'

'He's doing it for me. Isn't that wonderful?'

Miss Wilde closed her book. 'Yes, Lorelli, it is remarkable. It's unbelievable. I'm not sure I can process it immediately, but I am deeply indebted to you. As usual, I am in awe of such competence and such confidence in one so young. I don't know how to thank you.'

'You don't need to. I just want you to keep teaching me how to write.'

'Very well. Tell me about your Russian dressmaker. Any sign of chapter two?'

'It's hopeless. I don't know how to move the story on.'

Miss Wilde removed her glasses and sighed. 'Someone arrives, someone leaves, something is lost or something is found. Make things happen and the story will move on.'

'But how do I know if they are the right things?'

'You won't. You have to work to find the story. It is there. Your words will help you uncover it.'

'But you said I had to make things happen myself. Isn't that the opposite?'

'Yes, but you are not a scientist. Your methods don't have to make sense. You're a writer. They shouldn't make sense.'

'I don't think I am a writer,' said Lorelli sadly. 'I look at my characters' situations and I know what has to happen, but I don't know how to make it happen.'

'None of us walks one perfect path. Stories are like life. They are made up of each step. As a writer, all you need to do is document that journey with all its stumbles and trips. Make mistakes. Each one will make you better at what you do.'

'But when I read your book there were no mistakes. It felt as though everything happened to Franciska so perfectly.'

'Even though her life ends tragically? Remember, you never liked the ending of my book. You wanted to change it.'

'I understand now that it's perfect because it's true.'

Miss Wilde removed her glasses. 'Lorelli, no one bought my book. It went out of print.'

'So you gave up?'

'I didn't give up on writing. Writing gave up on me.'

'You keep telling me to believe in myself and write my story. You don't listen to your own advice.'

'When you get to my age you understand that advice is easier to give than take.'

'I don't believe that and I don't believe you do either. I want to be a writer, but you are one. Even if you have forgotten that.'

Miss Wilde placed a hand over Lorelli's. 'That's the thing about youth. They won't be told. And why should they? Refusing to do what you're told is the only way you'll ever achieve anything worth doing.'

A Pound of Flesh

Ovid was planning to spend a while at the bus stop, building up the courage to go in to see Millicent, but as he turned the corner he saw Father Whelan standing outside Hartwell's Rare Meat Emporium. He was flapping the wing-like sleeves of his tunic and waving a placard that read: 'A pound of flesh. The devil's butcher!'

'Stay away!' yelled the hysterical priest.

A passerby crossed the road to avoid him.

'Beware those who enter this house of sin. Shame on those who protect it,' he ranted at no one in particular.

His bloodshot eyes swivelled in their sockets and settled on Ovid. 'Ah, the Thornthwaite boy. Why am I not surprised to see you approach this terrible shop of death?'

'It's a butcher's,' said Ovid.

'This is no butcher's,' said Father Whelan. 'It is a den of devilry, a shop of horror, a business of Beelzebub.'

The door opened and Mr Hartwell stepped out. He wiped his hands on his stained apron and stood with fists on hips. Father Whelan stared back defiantly.

'Now, Father, let's not go through this again,' said Mr Hartwell.

'I must speak. I must be heard,' proclaimed Father Whelan. 'The villagers must be warned . . .'

Mr Hartwell took a step forward. Father Whelan shrank a little and tried to hide behind the placard.

'I have a reputable business with specialist clientele,' snarled Mr Hartwell.

'Clientele? Is that what they call Lucifer's cannibalistic hordes now?'

'Father Whelan, I have already called Sergeant Putnam. I suggest you move along before he is forced to make a report that will get back to the archbishop.'

'My superiors are as bad as the police. They are all establishment members who do nothing but protect people like you.'

'People like me?' Mr Hartwell crossed his arms.

'Your wife,' whispered Father Whelan. 'You killed her, then chopped her up and sold her as meat. How many more have you killed? How many more will you turn into mincemeat before you are stopped?'

'I can think of one more.' Mr Hartwell placed a hand on Father Whelan's shoulder.

The priest screamed and batted Mr Hartwell's hand away. 'Get off me, you fiend!'

Sergeant Putnam arrived. With his snugly fitted uniform, buttons straining to connect over his sizeable belly, he was not as intimidating a figure as Mr Hartwell, but, seeing him, Father Whelan finally lowered his placard.

'Morning, Fred,' said the policeman. 'Morning, Father. How are we today?'

'Apparently I am a murderer and you are in on it,' said Mr Hartwell.

Sergeant Putnam wagged his finger at Father Whelan. 'Now, Father Whelan, not this again.'

Father Whelan whispered, 'This meat is murder.'

'Where do you get these ideas?'

'I will not reveal my sources.' The crazed priest stared into the shop window.

'We've been through this. You can't just go around accusing people of killing their wives willy-nilly,' said Sergeant Putnam. 'You know perfectly well that Mrs Hartwell left, but instead of offering Mr Hartwell sympathy, you make these outlandish accusations. It's not good form, Father. Not good at all.'

Sergeant Putnam shook his head at the priest, as though scolding a misbehaving child. 'You're lucky that Mr Hartwell is more patient with you than I am. Now, move along.'

Father Whelan took a moment to glare at Mr Hartwell before turning and disappearing down the road, his tunic flapping behind him.

'You sure you don't want me to make an official charge?' said Sergeant Putnam.

'No, that's fine,' said Mr Hartwell. 'I just don't know where he gets these ideas in his head.'

'Too much altar wine is my guess.' Sergeant Putnam noticed Ovid. 'You're the Thornthwaite lad. The last time I came up your way was that unfortunate business with Mrs Bagshaw. How is she?'

'Hazel says she's been moved to a low-security prison,' replied Ovid.

'I'm pleased. It seems wrong putting away a sweet lady like that. You take care now. I'd better go and check Whelan makes it back to the vicarage without upsetting any more of the locals.' Sergeant Putnam ambled away in the same direction as the priest, leaving Mr Hartwell to turn to Ovid. 'I've a batch of wildebeest for your uncle,' he said.

'Wildebeest. Yum,' said Ovid.

Mr Hartwell pushed the door shut and lowered his head to speak in Ovid's ear. 'I know why you're here. I don't want you anywhere near my daughter. Everyone here knows about you and your family. Millicent has troubles enough. You're to stay away from her. Do you understand?'

Ovid could see Millicent inside the shop. From the look on her face she knew what her father was saying to him. Mr Hartwell went into the shop, picked up a package of meat and brought it out for Ovid.

'I don't want any misunderstanding,' he said. 'I am not warning you. I am threatening you. Stay away from my daughter. One thing I do agree with that deluded old priest about: you Thornthwaites are poison.'

Cricks' Glassware

A little bell tinkled as Lorelli stepped into Cricks' Glassware. It was a beautiful shop. The shelves were full of coloured glass ornaments of all shapes and sizes. There were bowls, jugs, glasses and other assorted objects. They caught the sunlight and painted the walls with vibrant colours. Felicia appeared at the back door. 'Oh Lori-chicken!' she cried. 'You've come, you've come . . . How lovely. Is Ovid with you too?'

'No. I think he's gone to see Millicent.'

'Oh.' Felicia's face fell into a pout. 'You don't think he really likes her, do you? Even if he does, he'll change his mind when he finds out how much better he can do.'

Felicia caught her reflection in a mirror and adjusted a stray strand of blonde hair. Lorelli felt a little queasy at the idea of Felicia being attracted to her brother, so she changed the subject. 'This place is amazing.'

'It's nothing compared to Thornthwaite Manor,' said Felicia. 'I'd give anything to swap places with you. Would you like to see the workshop? Mum and Dad are in there making things at the moment.'

Lorelli followed Felicia into the back room where there were rows of tools lining the walls. Mr and Mrs Crick were standing in front of a pair of furnaces. Mr Crick held a long pole, the other end of which was inside one of the furnaces. He turned it a few times, then pulled it out. He rested it on the metal bar, while Mrs Crick added molten glass to the end.

'Ah, a visit from our landlady. How lovely.' Mr Crick bowed.

'Honestly, Martin, stop teasing the poor girl,' said his wife.

'Why is it teasing?' asked Lorelli.

'This shop belongs to your estate,' explained Mr Crick. 'Half of the shop owners in town pay rent to you.'

'Ignore him,' said Mrs Crick. 'My husband switches off his brain when he's working.'

'Brain? What brain?'

Lorelli loved the way Felicia's parents spoke to each other. There was always such tenderness and warmth.

'What are you making?' she asked.

'We haven't decided yet,' said Mr Crick. 'Sometimes we just start and see where the glass takes us.'

'You sound like a hippy,' said Mrs Crick.

'I would be a hippy if I could grow the hair,' he replied.

Felicia brought Lorelli a chair and she sat down to watch them work. She enjoyed the warmth of the furnace and the contented glow of Mr and Mrs Crick's conversation. Occasionally Mr Crick asked his wife for something. Sometimes Mrs Crick would explain part of the process, but mostly they worked side by side without the need for words. When they had finished Mrs Crick opened an oven door and Mr Crick placed the vase they had made inside.

'Does it need to be cooked?' asked Lorelli.

'No, it needs to cool down,' said Mr Crick. 'But it needs to cool down very slowly. This is the cooling kiln. It cools the glass down gradually over thirty-six hours.'

'Why? What would happen if it didn't?'

'It would crack,' said Mrs Crick.

'More like explode,' said Mr Crick.

'And they're more difficult to sell like that,' said Mrs Crick. 'I'm going to make some coffee. Would you girls like some hot chocolate?'

'Oh yes,' said Felicia. 'Hot chocolate would be heaven, wouldn't it, Lori-chicken?'

'Heaven,' said Lorelli.

Artie Newly Is Dead

'This is sabotage! You 'ear me? Sabotage!'

Beaufort's words echoed around Thornthwaite Manor as he stormed down the corridor, yelling at the top of his voice.

The irate chef stopped at the bottom of the central staircase holding a frying pan in one hand and a bread knife in the other.

'My oxygen 'as been cut off. My blood has been sucked out. My breath has been stolen.'

Dragos appeared on the landing. He wore his yellow hard hat as usual and held a large spanner. 'What is all this shouting? You disturb the old lady with this noise.'

'The gas,' Beaufort hissed. 'Who is the culprit who turned off my gas?'

'I am culprit,' said Dragos.

'You?' cried the French chef. 'You are the saboteur. Well? What are you waiting for? Turn it back on again.'

'I will turn back on when I have finished job. I must put the old lady's needs first.'

'What old lady? What are you talking about? A building is not a living thing. It is a space in which an artist can create, but I cannot create without gas.'

'You can use the oven until it is back on,' said Dragos. 'Oven is electric.'

Beaufort's inhalation of breath sounded like an ocean pulling back before the next wave crashed onto the beach. 'An oven?' he cried. 'The art of cooking cannot be realised in a cave. My art is created upon the engines of creation. I must cook with gas. I must make smoke. I must have fire. Besides, I switched off the electricity in that part of the building.'

'You switched off electrics,' said Dragos. 'You are not allowed to do this. Why are you doing this?'

'Because of the fire alarm. *Beep, beep, beep*. All the time. *Beep, beep, beep*. So I tripped the fuse. Now, no more *beep, beep*.'

'This is dangerous. The fire alarm is there for good reason. You must not tamper.'

'How dare you?' yelled Beaufort.

'What on earth is going on?' Nurse Griddle stepped out of the library.

'*Madame*, this is none of your . . .' The rest of Beaufort's sentence died in his throat. It was the first time he had set eyes on her since his arrival.

'Artie?' Nurse Griddle peered at Beaufort as though she was looking at a face in an old photograph that had suddenly come to life and spoken.

'Eileen?' Beaufort stared back with equal bafflement and wonder. Guilt and shame played in his hazel eyes.

'You know each other?' asked Dragos.

'Artie Newly?' said Nurse Griddle, still struggling to speak.

164

'That has not been my name for many years,' said Beaufort.

'Who is this Artie Newly?' asked Dragos, clearly confused.

'Artie Newly is the man I was to marry before he drowned in Avernus Lake,' replied Nurse Griddle. 'Artie Newly is dead.'

A Small Favour

Considering the many perils of the Thornthwaite twins' upbringing, it was surprising that neither had ever set foot in Hexford Hospital before. Tom gave them a lift but waited in the car while they entered the large red-brick building and found a waiting room with harsh strip lighting. The whole place smelt of illness and medicine.

Ovid reached into his pocket and pulled out the carved tortoise.

'You went to see Millicent again yesterday, didn't you?' said Lorelli. 'How was it?'

Ovid was unsure what to say. It was a simple enough question, but to answer it honestly would have involved admitting to the crushing pain of rejection, the lingering sense of injustice and the profound sadness he felt.

'It was fine,' he said.

A young blonde-haired nurse entered the room, looked at them sympathetically, then informed them they could go through.

'Do you know what happened?' asked Lorelli.

'Your uncle had a heart attack,' replied the nurse.

'A heart attack?' repeated Lorelli. 'Are you sure? Did you check for poisoning?'

The nurse looked confused by this.

'Please excuse my sister,' said Ovid. 'She gets funny ideas in her head sometimes.'

'I see.' The nurse eyed Lorelli warily. 'Would you like to come through and see him now?' She led them into a room with softer lighting and flowers on the bedside table.

Uncle Harry was sitting up in bed reading. 'Lorelli, Ovid. How kind of you to come.'

'Are you all right?' asked Lorelli.

'Fit as a fiddle.' Uncle Harry closed the book and placed it on the bedside table.

'The nurse said you had a heart attack,' said Lorelli.

Uncle Harry swallowed. 'Yes. I have a heart condition. It turns out that Heartless Harry isn't heartless at all. He just has an incurably weak heart. It is my third attack. They tell me my next might be my last, but then they always say that.'

'You mean, you're dying?' said Lorelli.

'Yes,' said Uncle Harry.

'So that's what Mr Farthing was talking about,' said Ovid.

'You've been spying on me,' said Uncle Harry. 'I can't blame you. I should have come clean about it from the beginning.'

'Yes. Why didn't you?' asked Ovid.

'I was worried you would have no interest in getting to know me if you didn't think I had long to live.'

'That's an awful thing to think,' said Lorelli.

'I know,' said Uncle Harry. 'I still have a great deal to learn.' When he picked up the book from the bedside table, Lorelli recognised its blank cover.

'It's Alfred's book,' she said.

'Yes, I had it on me when I was brought here. It's been all I've had to read.' He opened it up onto a page with the heading:

Lord Willard Thornthwaite
1808–1838

'I was interested in this one because I've been staying in his room at the manor.'

'Wasn't he the terrible poet?' asked Ovid.

'He was,' replied Uncle Harry. 'But he was also the ancestor who came closest to escaping his fate. According to this, his mother wanted him to marry one girl but he ran off and had a secret wedding with another. He gave up his birthright for love.'

'Why are you telling us all this?' asked Lorelli.

'I thought it was interesting. For generations there were only single sons born into your family. Willard came the closest to smashing the constraints of the Thornthwaite legacy.'

'And what legacy would that be?' asked Ovid.

Uncle Harry turned to the title page. '*A History of Murder,*' he read out. 'Not something to be proud of. Willard wanted to break out and start afresh. You two have the chance to do the same. You have the chance to escape the expectations of your family name.'

'Escape with you?' said Ovid.

Uncle Harry closed the book and handed it to Lorelli. 'I won't lie. That is my hope. I have limited time. I want to spend it wisely.'

'Then you need to be honest with us from now on,' said Lorelli.

'About everything,' said Ovid. 'Including the reason why there is a leopard in the mine.'

'Oh, you've found out about Jenny,' said Uncle Harry. 'Yes, she's mine.'

'Jenny?' said the twins as one.

'I thought the mine would be a safe place to keep her. I had her delivered that day we visited the graveyard. Tom told me no one ever went down there.'

'Tom? Did he know?' said Lorelli.

'Not about the leopard.'

'What do you mean by that?' asked Ovid.

'It's not really my place to say, but think about it. Tom knew I existed, didn't he? They all did. All this time your servants knew about me and they never told you. I wonder why.'

'I'm more interested to know why you hid a leopard in our grandfather's mine,' said Lorelli.

Uncle Harry picked up a glass of water and took a sip. 'It turns out that doing the right thing is harder than I imagined. Do you remember me saying about the zoo?'

'The one you shut down for profit,' said Ovid.

'I did shut it down, but not for profit. It was the right thing to do. In those days there were fewer laws about zoo animal conditions. Your mother and I hated seeing those magnificent beasts locked up in those pokey cells. Martha used to cry about it at night. She was a sensitive soul, your mother.'

'What has this to do with the leopard?' asked Lorelli.

'I promised your mother that one day I would set them all free. I have now fulfilled that promise. I shut down that zoo and found good homes for all the animals, but there was a complication with Jenny. Her species is endangered so there are strict laws about where I'm allowed to release her. If she wasn't here, she would have been released into the wild, but Jenny was bred in captivity. She's never hunted. The wild would be as good as a death penalty. That's why I had her brought here and hidden.'

'In our mine?' said Ovid.

'I know it sounds crazy, but it's true. And I didn't tell you because the authorities are looking for her. She's a fugitive. I didn't want you to have to lie for me.'

Ovid looked at his sister and saw his own doubt reflected in her bottle-green eyes.

'I know it sounds unlikely,' said Uncle Harry, 'but I swear it's true.'

'What do you plan to do with Jenny now?' asked Lorelli.

'Honestly? I have no idea. This is a decision I made with my heart, not my head.'

'Your incurably weak heart?' said Ovid.

'Look, I know this is a lot to take in, but it's true. I promise with my hand on my incurably weak heart, from now on, no more lies.'

'Mr Hartwell gave me some wildebeest,' said Ovid. 'It's for Jenny, isn't it?'

'Yes, poor girl must be famished,' said Uncle Harry. 'Please could you ask Tom to take it down for her?'

'No. We'll do it,' said Ovid.

'It's too dangerous,' protested Uncle Harry. 'I must keep you safe.'

'You don't need to worry about us,' said Lorelli. 'We'll feed her.'

Uncle Harry took their hands in his. 'You're good kids,' he said. 'Such good kids.'

One's True Self

Nurse Griddle was in no doubt that the man standing in front of her was Artie Newly. His face had aged, his hair had thinned and he had grown a moustache, but there was no denying those eyes. The question of how a drowned man might return from the dead as a French chef had been neither answered, nor, as yet, asked.

'I am truly sorry,' said Beaufort. 'I never thought for a moment you would still be 'ere, Eileen. I thought it would be safe to return.'

It didn't take long for Nurse Griddle's shock and confusion to boil over into pure, unadulterated anger. 'Do you know how ridiculous you sound?' she cried.

'What can I say? There comes a time when an affectation becomes one's identity. Artie Newly died in that lake. This man who stands before you is Beaufort Nouveau.'

'What utter claptrap,' spat Nurse Griddle.

Beaufort smiled. 'You always did know how to put me in my place,' he said. 'Even now I am someone else.'

'I am still awaiting an explanation.'

'I was young. We were both young. I only asked you to marry me because you were pregnant. You said yes for the same reason. We were doing what people do. We were reacting to our situation. I could see my whole future mapped out before me. My life was to be one of survival. I felt trapped. I felt suffocated. I was already drowning before I jumped in that river.'

'So you faked your death?' said Nurse Griddle.

'It was not my intention. When I made that reckless bet with Dickie, I suppose a part of me was looking for a way out. Part of me wanted to drown. I came close too. The water was so cold my joints seized up. When a man comes so close to death he sees things differently. The lake did not claim my life. It gave me a chance to claim it for myself. I knew I could not go through with the wedding. There was too much I wanted to achieve. I could not see a way of doing it as Artie Newly, so I made whatever sacrifices necessary to live the life I desired.'

'I see,' said Nurse Griddle, her arms crossed. 'And so you ran off, acquired a French accent and became a chef. How thrilling for you.'

'I made many sacrifices to become what I am, but yes, I went to France. I was always good with languages and susceptible to other people's accents. I landed a dishwashing job in a restaurant, where I first learned what was possible with cooking. As I worked my way up from dishwasher to kitchen 'elp to sous chef to 'ead chef, I spoke only French. I became the man I wanted to be and gradually I forgot the man I 'ad been.'

'And you forgot the people you left behind,' said Nurse Griddle. 'So why come back now?'

'I 'ad no idea you were 'ere.'

173

'You must have known.'

'I swear.'

'All this time, we've been under the same roof. You must have heard my name.'

'What can I say?' said Beaufort. 'My art is all I care about. It absorbs my every fibre.'

'You are certainly coming across as self-absorbed,' said Nurse Griddle. 'Does Hazel know?'

''Azel . . . I . . . Of course. Yes, I . . .' Beaufort's French accent slipped a little as he struggled to find the words. 'She is mine?'

'She is most definitely not, but if you are asking if you are her father, then yes, you are.'

'I am sorry.' Beaufort looked at the floor and shuffled awkwardly. 'My obsession blinds me. My passion demands single-mindedness.'

'The word is selfishness. You must go now and never return.'

''Azel is a good girl,' said Beaufort.

Nurse Griddle stepped forward and looked down her nose at Beaufort. 'You will not speak her name. You will not hurt her. You will not take her away from me.'

'Take 'er away?' began Beaufort.

'You have obviously won over the poor girl, but she has had enough disruption in her life. And you have caused quite enough upset. I will not have you cause any more.'

'It was never my intention,' said Beaufort.

He turned and walked away. Nurse Griddle went back into the library. Neither saw Hazel sitting at the top of the stairs, listening to every word.

A Kind of Father

Hazel stopped outside the kitchen door. She could hear Beaufort sharpening the knives. She wondered why he would bother. They were not his knives. He had arrived with no implements and no ingredients and yet he had made miracles. She couldn't bear the thought of him leaving and everything going back to normal. She opened the door. He looked up from the knife. She could see his reflection in its blade.

''Azel,' he said. 'I'm afraid something has come up. I must leave.'

'I heard you,' said Hazel. 'I heard you both.'

'Oh.'

'I have a question.'

'Is it about the accent?'

'No. I want to know if it was because of me.'

'What?' asked Beaufort.

'Did you leave because of me?' Saying the words out loud drew tears from Hazel's eyes.

''Azel, no, I . . .' Beaufort's French accent wavered. 'It was because of me. It had nothing to do with you.'

'You told her you felt trapped.'

'Yes, you are right,' admitted Beaufort. 'But I did not know who you were. You were just an idea then. If I had known . . .'

'I don't blame you,' said Hazel. 'I should. I know I should, but I don't blame you. I know what it's like to feel suffocated. I understand the need to escape.'

Beaufort stopped what he was doing. ''Azel, I have been trying to explain. I am no father.'

'I don't want a father,' said Hazel. 'Two mothers is enough for anyone. I want a mentor. Take me on as your apprentice.'

Beaufort placed the knife down and stepped out from behind the kitchen counter. 'I wish I could, but I 'ave promised.'

'I don't care about her.'

'I am not a good man. I 'ave never desired to be a good man. I only strive to be a good artist. I have sacrificed everything for my art. Even you.'

Father and daughter stood in uncertain silence. A cold breeze blew through the kitchen. The hanging pots rattled and the dishcloth flapped. Hazel and Beaufort turned to see Mrs Bagshaw standing in the doorway.

'Oh hello, Hazel, my love, be a dear and pop the kettle on, would you? I don't know what kind of tea they serve in that place but it is not the good kind. I could murder a proper cup of tea.'

Mrs Bagshaw stepped into the kitchen as though she had never been away. Seeing her mother, Hazel ran into her arms.

'Mum,' she wept. 'Mum.'

'There, there,' whispered Mrs Bagshaw. 'I'm back now. They let me out. Everything is going to be all right.'

By the time Hazel remembered about Beaufort, he was gone.

ACT III

Bleeding Hearts

Ovid stared out of the back window as Tom navigated the country lanes at a painfully slow pace. The package of wildebeest meat on the seat next to him was a cold, stinking reminder of the morning's events. Lorelli was up front, clutching Alfred Crutcher's book.

'You see all these trees lining this road?' said Tom, slowing down for a corner so much that the car behind had to slam on its brakes to avoid a crash.

Neither twin responded. They weren't in the mood for one of Tom's horticultural musings.

'They're all the same age as me. How do you suppose I know that?'

'I have no idea,' said Ovid, 'but I daresay you'll tell us.'

'Because they were planted on the same day I was born. My father told me that. Maybe that's the reason I've always felt better disposed to these trees than to most. I expect you two feel that way about each other. There's something special about sharing a birthday, isn't there?'

Lorelli caught Ovid's gaze in the wing mirror. She had seen the same spark in his eyes before. It usually appeared just before he executed one of his deadly attempts on her life. Or just before she did. Ovid was plotting something or he was working out a plot against someone.

'Could you drop us off at the mine, please, Tom?' said Ovid.

'You'll steer clear of that mine if you've got any sense,' said Tom. 'It's not safe.'

'If you're referring to the leopard then we already know,' said Lorelli.

'Ah. Is that what it is?' said Old Tom.

'You knew?' said Ovid.

'I knew there was something down there. I did not know it was a leopard.'

'You didn't think to tell us?'

'I assumed you knew.'

'What else do you assume we know?' said Lorelli.

'Lots of things.'

'Like what?'

'I assume you know that Silas's mine is far too dangerous to be messing about in, leopard or no leopard.'

'It's fine. I used to go down there loads,' said Ovid.

'I know, and I warned you against it back then too. I've lived to see two Thornthwaites meet their ends in that mine. I'd rather not see any more go that way.'

'You mean Lord Silas and his first wife?' said Lorelli.

'That's right.' Tom kept his eyes firmly on the road.

'I saw a film called *Hotel Nowhere* this week,' said Ovid.

'*Hotel Nowhere*? Now that takes me back,' said Old Tom with a wistful sigh. 'Yes, I remember them coming to make it. Can't say I ever saw it.'

'There was a man in it who looked like Dragos,' said Ovid.

'Really?' repeated Lorelli. It was the first time her brother had mentioned this.

'The film was made sixty years ago,' said Tom. 'That's quite a bit older than Dragos.'

'Sixty years?' said Ovid. 'But I saw a boy in the window. I assumed it was our father.'

'Your father would have been forty-seven this coming July if he had lived,' said Tom. 'No, back then the only young lad living on the estate was me, so I guess it must have been me you saw. Now, about this leopard. It would be better if I were to feed it.'

'We promised Uncle Harry we'd do it,' said Lorelli.

'It's a funny sort of uncle who would put his nephew and niece in danger.'

'You don't like him, do you?' said Lorelli.

'I don't especially know him,' said Tom.

'Why didn't you tell us about him?' asked Lorelli. 'You knew about him. You must have met him before, when he came to our parents' wedding.'

'I wouldn't say met, but, yes, I knew of him.'

'But you never told us about him. Did you assume we knew about him too?' asked Lorelli.

'No.' Tom pointed to some pink flowers along the side of the road under a tree, with drooping heads. 'You see those beauties?' he said. 'They're called Bleeding Hearts. Lovely little delicate things with their curved stems and heads always bowed. I always think of you two when I see them.'

'Why? Because they look sad?' said Lorelli.

'They don't look sad to me. They look thoughtful,' said Tom. 'But, no, it's not that. It's just that they grow in the shade. Too much light and they wither and die.'

'What does that mean?' asked Ovid.

'It means some things grow when they're kept in the shadows.'

Peril in the Mine

Lorelli could pinpoint the first moment she understood that her life was different to other people's. A man from the gas board had come to read the meter and only narrowly avoided being pelted by tarantulas. Lorelli could still remember his cries as he ran from the house.

'What's wrong with you people? You're deranged. You're not normal!'

His words came back to her now as she and Ovid traipsed through the damp undergrowth, carrying the bag of raw wildebeest meat to feed the fugitive leopard in the mine. It was not normal, and yet, for Lorelli, the growing feeling of disquiet and distrust felt like the most natural thing in the world.

She wanted so badly to trust Ovid, but how could she trust anyone? Tom and Uncle Harry were not the only ones with secrets. Sometimes she felt as though the only person she could trust was Adam Farthing, and he was currently seeing a specialist about his habitual lying.

'I hate it,' said Lorelli as they reached the lift shaft. 'How did it get like this again?'

'It's our first leopard, isn't it?' said Ovid casually. 'We had the bear and a few snakes . . . and wasn't there a crocodile in the hothouse once?'

'I'm not talking about a specific species of animal. I'm talking about all this dishonesty. Why are none of us capable of telling the truth?'

'All right.' Ovid stepped into the life. 'Let's be honest. You've been scared of the dark ever since that thing with the cupboard and the snake, haven't you?'

'I don't know what you're talking about. I can barely remember that,' said Lorelli firmly.

She joined him inside the lift.

'Tom's right,' said Ovid. 'We're more suited to dark than light.' He slid the door shut and the lift rattled down. 'I used this place as a base back when I was building a killer freezer,' he said with a nostalgic sigh.

'I don't remember a killer freezer.'

'It never worked properly.'

'You mean it didn't kill?'

'Oh, it would have killed fine, but it didn't keep food cold and that was all part of the plan.'

The lift came to a standstill at the bottom of the shaft and Ovid held the gas lamp, then waved the package of meat. 'Jenny! Jenny?' he called. 'Where is she then?'

'Let's just throw it and go,' said Lorelli.

'Where's the fun in that? Look, here she comes.' A pair of keen eyes appeared in the dark and the leopard made its way silently towards them. Ovid dangled the wildebeest meat. She growled. He dropped it. The leopard sniffed the package then settled down to eat and Ovid reached out his hand and tickled her behind her ears. The leopard made a little satisfied purr as she sank her teeth into the soft flesh.

'Ovid, I'm going up, with or without you,' said Lorelli.

'Spoilsport,' he replied, but he joined her in the lift. Lorelli pressed the UP button. Nothing happened. She pressed it again. Still nothing.

'What's wrong?' asked Ovid.

'It's not working.'

'Let me try.' Ovid took the control and pressed the button. 'It's packed in. Don't worry. There's a ladder that comes up at the bottom of the croquet field. Come on, we'd probably better get moving before Jenny finishes dinner and starts thinking about pudding.'

'Can't you fix the lift?' said Lorelli.

'Are you sure you're not scared of the dark?' asked Ovid.

'No. I'm fine. Let's go while she's still busy with that meat.'

As the twins edged around her, Lorelli felt the soft brush of Jenny's fur against her leg. Once past, they sped up. Ovid held the lamp. Lorelli was close behind.

'You're waving that thing around too much,' said Lorelli. They rounded another corner and she felt her foot kick something. She bent down and found an old tin hat. She picked it up and switched on the torch. 'It still works.'

'I know. You're shining it in my eyes,' said Ovid.

She placed it on her head. 'What's that sound?'

Behind them the leopard was growling, either in satisfaction or having got the taste for even fresher meat. The twins sped up, running as fast as the twisting tunnels allowed.

'She's getting closer.' Lorelli felt as though the walls were closing in on her. The light on her hat should have helped but the shifting shadows fed her imagination. Fear gripped her like a hand to the throat. She struggled to breathe. Her chest tightened.

'This is it. This is our way out.' Ovid started to climb. Lorelli followed. From the loudness of the growl, she could tell the leopard was getting close. Lorelli followed her brother up. It felt like he was climbing too slowly.

'Ovid, you're right. I am scared of the dark,' she said. 'And of being eaten by leopards. Climb faster.'

The leopard was beneath them. When it growled, it sounded like thunder. It jumped up, its jaws snapping at Lorelli's feet. She could feel its breath, warm and with the rich stench of raw wildebeest.

'Ovid, climb quicker!' she yelled.

The leopard jumped again.

She snatched the hard hat off her head and took aim. As she did she caught a glimpse of the name written on the back. *Vāduva.*

The leopard was on its hind legs with its eyes focused on its prey. It was about to jump. It would reach high enough this time. Lorelli lobbed the hat. It smacked the leopard right between the eyes as it was about to spring. Finally, Jenny fell back to the ground and the twins climbed up towards the light.

Mrs Bagshaw's
Turnip Soup

There are people who would have let out exclamations of joy and relief after such a narrow escape from death. Most people, probably. The Thornthwaite twins were not most people. They stepped onto the croquet pitch, brushed themselves down and continued on their way back to the manor.

Ovid said, 'Tom really does keep this pitch in immaculate order. We should have a game one day soon now it's getting warmer.'

'I remember the last game we had,' said Lorelli. 'You set fire to Tom's rose bushes.'

'Was that the paraffin croquet balls?' said Ovid.

'No, hot coals dropped from the southwest tower.' Lorelli looked up and spotted Dragos working on the tower. 'You said you saw someone who looked like Dragos in that old film.'

'Yes, but Tom's right. He's not old enough,' said Ovid.

'That mining helmet had his surname on it,' said Lorelli.

'Maybe he's been doing some repairs down there,' said Ovid.

'The helmet hadn't been used in years. Besides, you know what he's like about safety. He would never leave it down there if it was his.'

Ovid pushed down a molehill with his heel. 'Now I think about it, Tom never denied it. He said the film was too old, then changed the subject.'

'So, what? It was a relation of Dragos's?'

'Maybe.'

'It doesn't make sense. Why wouldn't he tell us? Why would he lie?'

'Why do any of them lie?' asked Ovid.

Up high on the tower, Dragos spotted them and waved. Lorelli raised a hand. With the sun going down behind him, Dragos's features were hidden in dark shadow.

'Maybe Silas was right. Maybe there really is gold down there.'

'Dragos has never shown any interest in that mine,' said Ovid.

They stepped in through the back door of the manor. Ovid held the door open for his sister. They heard a bell tinkle. Dinner was ready. They made their way to the dining room, where they found Hazel placing a vat of brown soup in the centre of the table. She removed the lid and a stench filled the room.

'Beaufort is off his game today,' said Ovid.

'Mrs Bagshaw made it,' said Hazel flatly.

'Mrs Bagshaw?' repeated the twins.

'Yes. She's back. She was released yesterday on good behaviour.'

'She was serving a fourteen-year sentence for murder,' exclaimed Ovid. 'How well behaved could she be?'

'I'm sorry, I don't know, sir . . .' Hazel was fighting hard not to cry and her voice wavered.

Seeing how upset she looked, Lorelli took her hand and said, 'You must be so relieved.'

'Yes, miss, I am . . . It's just . . . It's just . . .' She burst into tears and ran out of the room.

'I wonder what's wrong with her,' said Ovid.

He picked up a ladle and poured some soup into a bowl. He offered it to Lorelli, but she scowled at him. 'Hazel is obviously really upset and all you can think about is soup.'

Ovid lifted a spoonful of it, sniffed it, then poured it back in. 'Actually, I'd rather not think about this soup,' he said.

Tom Paine entered the room and sniffed. 'Ah, now there is a familiar smell,' he said. 'Mrs Bagshaw has requested that I join you for dinner. She's keen for me to try this soup of hers.'

'Tom,' said Lorelli, 'is everything all right? Hazel seemed rather upset.'

'That's on account of our French chef turning out to be a chap by the name of Artie Newly who, as it happens, is Hazel's father.' Tom poured himself a bowl of soup and picked up a rock-hard bread roll. He banged it on the table in a futile attempt to break through the crust. When it remained undamaged, he dipped it into the soup to soften it up.

'Her father?' said Lorelli. 'Did you know this?'

'I did think he had a familiar look to him, but no, I can't say I knew Artie well enough to recognise him after all these

189

years. Remember, Nurse Griddle didn't come to work here until after he was gone. How was the mine?'

'The lift packed in,' said Lorelli.

'I did warn you it's not safe down there, but I am relieved you made it out. If only to help me get through all this soup.'

'Tom, was it a relation of Dragos's I saw in that film?' asked Ovid.

Tom blew on a spoonful of soup and took a sip. He gulped it down and said, 'What makes you say that?'

'I found a helmet,' said Lorelli.

Tom muttered something inaudible, then spoke. 'Dragos's father worked for Silas.'

'Why didn't you tell us?' demanded Lorelli.

'And don't say you assumed we knew,' added Ovid. 'You vetted him before suggesting we take him on.'

Tom laid down his spoon and placed his elbows on the table, resting his chin on his hands. 'I kept it from you because I knew you would get like this.'

'Like what?' asked Ovid.

'Suspicious. I knew you'd go concocting your whodunnits and what-have-yous. But Dragos is a good, honest man and he cares for this house as much as any of us. He cares for you two as well. The fact that his father worked for your grandfather should make no difference.'

'We're not Bleeding Hearts,' said Lorelli. 'We deserve the truth.'

'The truth isn't something anyone deserves,' said Tom. 'It's something people earn.'

Fear of Telephones

Dragos had located an old-fashioned black-handled telephone in the attic and placed it on a three-legged table at the top of the main staircase in case of emergencies. As far as Ovid was concerned, no one knew the number, so when it rang later that evening he was slow to realise what the sound was. As his room was nearer, he reached it before his sister, but he was unaware that Lorelli had stopped just short of the corner to listen in on his side of the conversation.

He hesitated. His hand hovered over the ringing telephone. The twins' mother had been killed when she had answered the telephone during a thunderstorm. A lightning bolt had struck at the moment she picked up the receiver, frying the late Lady Thornthwaite. This had left Ovid with an understandable fear of telephones. He listened for any sign of thunder before cautiously picking up.

'Yes? Hello?' he said.

'Ovvy . . . it's me . . . Millicent,' a voice whispered.

'How did you get this number?'

'Lorelli gave it to me, but listen, I can't talk for long. My father might come in. He says I can't see you, but I don't care. Come and meet me tomorrow.' It was a bad line. Her voice sounded muffled.

'Meet you where?'

'The old water mill by Bagshaw's End at eleven o'clock. There are things I need to explain.'

'What things?'

'Things I need to say in person. I'll see you tomorrow.'

The line went dead and Ovid replaced the receiver. He remained by the phone, listening for a sign that anyone was eavesdropping. Satisfied that he was alone, he headed back towards his bedroom, only to bump into Hazel on the way. She was carrying a bundle of clean bed linen along the north corridor.

'Good evening, sir,' she said.

'Hazel,' he replied, 'Tom told us about Beaufort. It must have been . . . well, quite a shock.'

'Yes, sir. It was something of a shock.'

'It's funny in a way. Our uncle and your father turn up together.'

'It doesn't feel funny at the moment, sir.'

'No, I mean . . . No, you're right.'

Ovid had lived under the same roof as Hazel his entire life. She was only a year older, but Ovid could count the number of proper conversations they'd had on one hand.

'I heard the phone ring,' said Hazel. 'It was Millicent, wasn't it?'

'How did you know that?'

'You're smiling, sir.' Seeing his reaction, she said, 'I'm sorry. I didn't mean to speak out of turn.'

'There is nothing to say.'

'Yes, sir. Good night then, sir.'

'You know, you don't really need to call me sir,' said Ovid.

'Thank you, but Mrs Bagshaw is back now and she prefers it if I do, sir.'

'And Beaufort?'

'He's gone now, sir.'

'For good?'

'It doesn't feel good, but yes, sir. Forever.'

Ovid was not a natural reader of people, but it was easy enough to recognise emotions that had been so present in his own childhood. He understood fear and paranoia, but it was not either of these things that was plaguing Hazel. From the faraway look in her eyes to her quiet, tearful voice, Ovid understood that she was grieving.

Where to Start?

After listening in on Ovid's conversation, Lorelli waited until he went back to his room before returning to her own. She sat down at her desk, picked up a fresh sheet of white paper and a pen. In spite of Miss Wilde's encouragement, she had lost faith in her story about the Russian dressmaker. The character had seemed so vivid at first. Now, she felt flat and dull. Lorelli needed to write a story she believed in. She needed to be swept off her feet just as she had been when she first read *The Seven Dances of Franciska T'oth*. She didn't accept Miss Wilde's claim that a writer was in control. She believed that stories should spill out of a pen onto the page.

The white paper stared back at her. No more beginnings. Miss Wilde was right about that. She needed a story with a middle and an end too. Lorelli's pen hovered over the paper. Slowly she lowered it until its nib touched the white paper. She wrote the words:

Beginning, middle, end.

She stared at the words, then released her pen and dropped her head into her hands. Why was it so hard to find a story when she was surrounded by them? She picked up Alfred's book, *A History of Murder*. So many stories. Irony and tragedy. Love and death. But how did you know where a story started? Where was the beginning of her life story? Did it begin on the day of her birth or did it go further back than that? She put the book down and picked up the pen again. She found a fresh piece of paper and wrote: *How does a history of murder end?* Then she wrote the answer. *When everyone is dead.* She crushed the paper into a ball and threw it across the room. She considered writing to Adam, but she had promised him only the truth and Lorelli was no longer sure she knew what that was.

She gave up and went to bed but struggled to sleep. When she did finally drift off it was into a disturbed slumber. The next morning she entered the dining room, bleary-eyed and groggy-headed. She found Ovid staring at a mountain of dry black puddings. There was a big black pan of baked beans, piles of burnt toast, soggy bacon stacked high and greasy fried eggs with solid yolks. Mrs Bagshaw entered with a bowl of boiled mushrooms.

'Ah, my young masters, Lorelli and Ovid. How lovely to see you. Please don't stand on ceremony. It all needs to be eaten. Tuck in. Tuck in.'

'Mrs Bagshaw, welcome home,' said Lorelli.

'Thank you, dear, but the best welcome you can give me is a full stomach. Come on now, eat up.'

Not wanting to cause offence, Lorelli placed a sausage, an egg and a piece of toast on her plate, while Ovid risked the mushrooms.

'So, how was prison?' asked Ovid.

'An experience better forgotten,' said Mrs Bagshaw. 'If I hadn't had my turnips, I don't know what I would have done. They really helped me get away from it all.'

'Thank goodness for the turnips then,' said Ovid.

'Yes, but that's enough about me. What's new with you?' Mrs Bagshaw sat down at the table. 'Hazel has been hopeless at providing news. She keeps bursting into tears. I think she's a bit overwhelmed about my release. I'm sure you have bags to tell me.'

Worse Than
Murder

Ovid regretted the mushrooms. He was reminded of them with every bump he went over on the road to Little Fledgling. He cycled harder and sped up past Hartwell's Rare Meat Emporium, then parked his bike outside the old water mill and went around the side of the building. The mill had been out of use for as long as anyone could remember, but the large wooden wheel still turned during the wetter months when the stream flowed fast and high. Ovid leaned over the fence and gazed down at the swirling water. The rushing was so loud it took him a moment to realise someone was behind him.

'I've always loved it here. It's so pretty.'

He turned, expecting to see Millicent, but found Felicia standing behind him, wearing a pretty bow in her hair, a blue dress and an excited look on her face.

'Where's Millicent?' he asked.

'Oh, probably working in that dreadful meat shop, elbow deep in ox blood or some such horror. It's so icky.'

'But the phone call . . .'

'That was me, silly. I know you think you like her, so I pretended to be her, but it was me all along. Are you impressed?'

'Why would I be impressed that you lied to me?'

'Oh, Ovvy-wovvy, don't be like that. I pretended. I didn't lie. It's very different. And just think, one day it will be a cute story about how we started going out.'

Ovid racked his brain for a suitable response. His brain offered up nothing.

Felicia took a step closer. 'I know you think that someone like me would never look at someone like you, but you're wrong. I am looking at you.' She took a step closer. 'I've seen you.'

It felt like a well-rehearsed speech. There was something unnerving about the way she looked at him. Ovid moved back instinctively and his fingertips found the top of the wooden fence. It wobbled.

'What are you up to?' he said.

'Little old me? I'm not up to anything.' Another step.

'But Millicent . . .'

'Millicent isn't here now. I'm here.'

'You . . .'

The fear Ovid felt was unlike any he had previously experienced. It was almost as though he wanted Felicia to push him into the water. He made no effort to step away. He couldn't have moved if he had wanted to. His head was filled with the sound of rushing water.

'What do you want?' he said.

'I thought that was obvious.' Felicia took a baby step.

'I think we've always been mean to each other because deep down we like each other. That's quite common. It's always happening in books. But then, when you burst through that bathroom door and saved my life, I saw the real you. You are my hero.' She placed her hand flat on his chest so she could feel his heart beating. She closed her eyes and leaned in. Ovid realised to his horror that she was not about to push him into the water. She wasn't going to kill him. It was worse than that. She was going to kiss him. With equal bewilderment and disgust, he discovered he was going to let her.

A Two-way Kiss

Lorelli had kept her bicycle a secret from Ovid, so it was easy enough to follow him to Little Fledgling. She watched him park, then found a spot where she could observe but not hear his encounter with Felicia. When it came to the kiss, Lorelli found it embarrassing to watch. She turned to leave, only to find Millicent standing silently behind her.

'I hate her,' she said, staring at Felicia and Ovid. 'She knew I liked him. I hate them both.'

'Come on.' Lorelli placed an arm over her shoulder and led her away. 'He's just confused.'

'He didn't look confused.'

They took a bridge over the river. Millicent stopped halfway and kicked a stone into the water. She looked down at the ripple.

'It was only a kiss,' said Lorelli.

'You saw it. It wasn't just her kissing him. He kissed her.'

'He's an idiot,' admitted Lorelli. 'He had to read a bunch of books to work out what to do on his date with you. He wrote up his findings like it was a science project.'

Millicent showed no sign of amusement.

'Do you think he likes her?'

'No. He can't stand her.'

Millicent snorted. 'I know how he feels.'

'Millicent, as much as it pains me to say it, my brother isn't a bad person. Not really.'

'Isn't he?' demanded Millicent. 'He's spent his life trying to kill you.'

'What do you mean?' said Lorelli, stunned. 'Why would you say that?'

'Oh come on. Everyone knows. You're the Thornthwaite twins. It's what you do.'

'Everyone?' Millicent's words rang in Lorelli's ears like a tolling bell. All this time, she had been under the impression that their murderous past was a secret. Could it be true that the world knew? 'But . . . if you knew, why did you want to be my friend?'

'I didn't. Felicia made me. It was part of her stupid plan.' They stopped on a corner and waited for an elderly couple to pass.

'What plan?' asked Lorelli. 'What are you talking about?'

'She wanted to befriend you so she could get her hands on your inheritance. I was supposed to win over Ovid while she took care of you.'

'Took care of me?'

'Took care of you,' echoed Millicent darkly. 'She was using me to get to Ovid because she couldn't bear the thought of being near him herself.' Millicent snorted. 'She seems to have changed her mind about that.'

'What are you talking about?' asked Lorelli.

'That night with the chandelier, we were in the house too.

She disappeared to go to the toilet just before it happened. And the glass statue, that was all her idea. It was all part of the plan.'

'And you went along with all this?' said Lorelli.

'No. I didn't know how crazy she was.' Millicent tapped her head to indicate that Felicia was mad. 'It was just a game. As soon as I understood she was serious, I told her I would have nothing to do with it. That's when she turned on me. She got Dad to scare Ovid away, then she took him for herself.'

'Felicia? I don't believe it.'

'It's an act. All of it. I'd watch your back if I were you.'

'What do you mean?'

Millicent put on a baby voice to imitate Felicia. *'Ovvy-wovvy, wouldn't it be cosier with just the two of us? Wouldn't it be nicer if Lori-chicken's goose was cooked?'*

Back to Normal

Ovid and Lorelli were not alone in feeling that life at Thornthwaite Manor had returned to normal. Hazel stood in the kitchen, slowly stirring a pan of Mrs Bagshaw's winter vegetable soup. It did not smell good. She missed Beaufort. She felt terrible for admitting this even to herself, but it wasn't the same without him. Mrs Bagshaw's bland food had been bearable before Hazel understood the full possibilities of a kitchen. Her taste buds had been awakened. Her eyes had been opened.

Mrs Bagshaw hummed to herself as she diced carrots, oblivious to Hazel's guilt and despair. Nurse Griddle stepped into the kitchen and wrinkled her large, cavernous nose.

'Mrs Bagshaw,' she said, 'what a relief it is to have you back at the manor.'

'Why thank you, Nurse Griddle,' responded Mrs Bagshaw. 'It's a pleasure to be back.'

'Hazel has missed you terribly.'

It was true. Hazel had missed her mum. Mrs Bagshaw had always been there for her. Her relentless cheerfulness in the face of so much darkness had been as constant and reassuring as the sun in the sky.

'Oh, Eileen,' said Mrs Bagshaw. 'I am very grateful to you for looking after her during my stay away.'

'I have done very little,' said Nurse Griddle honestly. 'But tell me of your release. Tom said it was your turnips that sealed the deal.'

'That's right,' replied Mrs Bagshaw. 'I made one of my special soups, and it went down so well that the prison governor immediately allowed me out. Isn't that marvellous?'

'It's certainly remarkable,' said Nurse Griddle.

Mrs Bagshaw leaned over Hazel's shoulder, grabbed her hand and made her stir faster. 'That's it, my girl. Keep it moving. We don't want lumps for the young masters.' She turned to Nurse Griddle. 'How are they? They seemed a little subdued to me. Hazel has been telling me about their uncle putting them in his will.'

'Yes,' said Nurse Griddle. 'Obviously Tom and I have our concerns about his motives, but the young masters must be allowed to make their own decisions.'

'What if they choose to go and live with their uncle?' said Hazel.

Both her mothers turned to look at her.

'Why on earth would they decide to do such a thing?' asked Nurse Griddle.

'Perhaps they fear waking up one day and discovering that they have wasted their lives in this place,' said Hazel pointedly.

Nurse Griddle's eyes narrowed. 'Are we really talking about them?'

Hazel released the spoon. It spun round, then disappeared beneath the surface of the liquid. 'Why did you make him go away?' she said.

'Make who go away?' said Mrs Bagshaw.

'You deserve better than him,' said Nurse Griddle, ignoring her.

'Than who?' asked Mrs Bagshaw.

'There's no one better than him,' said Hazel. 'I want to be like him.'

'You want to run away from your responsibilities like he did?' said Nurse Griddle. 'You want to be as selfish as he has been. Is that it?'

'You were the one who said I had to make something of my life!' Hazel was screaming now. 'I don't want you. I want to go with my father.'

'Father?' said Mrs Bagshaw. 'What father?'

'Artie Newly,' said Nurse Griddle.

'His name is Beaufort Nouveau,' said Hazel. 'I want to go with him. I want to become a chef like him.'

Nurse Griddle took a step closer and said in a voice that sizzled with quiet anger, 'That man is not your father. He lost that chance when he left you.'

'So did you!' shouted Hazel, running from the kitchen to find somewhere quiet to weep.

Glassworks Death Trap

Lorelli stood outside Cricks' Glassworks, staring at her reflection in an ornately framed circular mirror. She thought about what Millicent had said. She wondered if it could possibly be true about Felicia. No, she couldn't believe it. Felicia was too vain to be scheming. She was too silly. Too Felicia. Millicent had either misunderstood or she was jealous. But that didn't change the fact that everyone knew the truth about the Thornthwaite twins.

All this time, Lorelli had tried so hard to keep her past hidden, but everyone knew; the postman on his bicycle, the window cleaner, the young family walking past. Across the road, she saw a curtain twitch, and Lorelli suddenly felt very conspicuous. She stepped into the shop to hide.

'Hello, Lorelli,' said Mrs Crick. 'If you're after Felicia, I'm afraid she's out. You're welcome to sit and wait for her. I'm sure she won't be long. As you can see, we're hardly rushed off our feet.'

The shop was empty, apart from the shelves of glassworks. To Lorelli, they looked more like rows of deadly weapons. She tried to shake the thought from her head.

'Are you all right?' asked Mrs Crick.

'Yes, sorry, I'm just a bit cold,' she said quietly.

'You're welcome to come through to the workshop to warm up.'

'Thank you.' Lorelli followed her inside. The warmth of the burning furnaces made her feel light-headed.

'Are you making anything at the moment?' she asked.

'No. The cooling kiln is full. I've got some errands to run and my husband is upstairs in the flat. Actually, would you mind keeping an eye on the shop for five minutes while I pop out? That way he won't have to inflict his pyjamas on an unsuspecting world.'

'Of course. That's fine.'

Mrs Crick plucked her coat from a hook. 'Thank you, Lorelli. You're a lovely girl, and, may I say, I think you're doing Felicia the world of good.'

'What do you mean by that?'

Mrs Crick bit her lip. 'Just that it's good to see her so content. So happy.'

'Isn't she always like that?'

'It doesn't seem like it to us, but then we're parents. It's our job to worry.'

'What do you worry about?'

Mrs Crick pulled a pair of tatty gloves from her pocket and placed them by the till. 'Martin and I have never put much value on money. We wouldn't have gone into this business if we had. But Felicia is different. I don't know why. Martin thinks it's all those books she reads about silly rich kids having jolly adventures. But I don't know if that's true. I think it's because rebelling is what children do. Show them one way, they'll find another.'

'You're saying she only cares about money?' said Lorelli, thinking about what Millicent had said about Felicia.

'Yes, but being friends with you, she's getting to see what it's really like being that rich.' Mrs Crick picked up a set of keys from a bowl. 'She can see that money doesn't buy you happiness.'

'You don't think I'm happy?' The heat making Lorelli feel giddy. She steadied herself on a chair.

'I think you're real. And real is much more complicated. So, I'll be back in a minute. Make yourself comfortable.'

Lorelli sat down and stared into the burning furnaces. She imagined half-formed faces and dancing figures in the flames. She remembered the last time she had stared with such intensity into a fire. A year ago, when she had watched her family home go up in flames. The fire brigade had arrived and Thornthwaite Manor had endured, but she still remembered that feeling of liberation as she had watched it burn.

When the shop bell rang it made Lorelli jump. She tried the connecting door, but it was locked from the other side. She wiggled the handle.

'Hello?' she called.

There was no response.

'Felicia? Mrs Crick?'

Nothing.

The bulb overhead went off, meaning the only light was that of the soft orange glow from the fire. *CLICK*. The cooling kiln door popped open. Lorelli could see the newly made glassworks inside. The sound of a crack brought to mind Mr Crick's words – that if the glass cooled too quickly it would explode. There were so many, the explosion would fill the room with broken glass. She rattled the connecting door but it would not open.

'Help!' she shouted. 'Is anyone there?'

It was no use. Lorelli looked around the room. There was no other way out. There was nowhere to hide. Lorelli pulled a hairclip from her hair and fiddled with the lock. She tried to focus on the job, ignoring thoughts of her impending death.

She knew from experience that it took time to pick a lock with a hairclip, so she was surprised and relieved when the door swung open. Mr Crick took her hand and pulled her out of the workshop. He slammed the door behind them as the glass in the workshop exploded, causing the whole building to shake. The glass ornaments that filled the shop tinkled and clinked as they wobbled precariously on the shelves. A tall vase on a shelf above Lorelli toppled. She caught it and handed it to Mr Crick.

'Thank you,' he said. 'Are you all right?'

'Yes, I think so.'

'What happened?'

'I don't know,' replied Lorelli. 'I think it was the power.' Mr Crick tried a light switch. 'The power cut must have triggered the oven door to open. I'm so sorry. There's supposed to be a back-up generator.'

'The door was locked.'

'The latch must have come off. Are you sure you're all right?'

'I'm fine,' said Lorelli. 'I'm leaving.'

'You shouldn't go anywhere. You're in shock. I'm sure Felicia will be back in a minute.'

Lorelli had known enough death traps to understand that she was on the wrong end of one. There was no doubt about it. Someone was trying to kill her and, given the circumstances, it seemed pretty clear who that someone was. Felicia Crick.

'I have to go,' she said, and she was out of the door before Mr Crick could stop her.

A Fugitive

Ovid's research into the world of dating had taught him that his first kiss should leave him feeling, as one rather wordy author had put it, 'as light as a feather fluttering on a gentle summer's breeze'. This had proved inaccurate. Ovid did not feel light. He felt heavy. Anxiety gripped him. Ovid's first kiss had been with Felicia Crick. The girl he thought he liked had rejected him. The girl he thought he hated had kissed him. It was confusing and deeply troubling.

On top of this, there was a good chance that someone was trying to kill him and his sister. The timing of the chandelier incident had coincided with Uncle Harry's arrival, but Ovid couldn't work out what he would stand to gain. The estate would go to Old Tom and Nurse Griddle if the twins were killed. Besides, Uncle Harry was rich enough as it was. But if life at Thornthwaite Manor had taught him anything, it was that no one was above suspicion: Old Tom, Nurse Griddle, Mrs Bagshaw, the Farthings, Uncle Harry, Hazel. Ovid couldn't even trust his own sister, but Lorelli was not his current prime suspect. Dragos Vaduva had the skillset to create the traps, he had the access and, if he believed there was gold in that old mine, he had the motive.

Then again, perhaps the whole thing was in his mind. Had he spent so long under a cloak of paranoia that he saw conspiracies and plots where there were none?

As Ovid freewheeled down the gravel driveway towards Thornthwaite Manor, he spotted Dragos walking up the hill in the direction of the old mine. He wore his hard hat and was carrying a bag over his shoulder. He was about to follow when Lorelli stepped out of the stables.

'Jolly fun morning?' she asked.

'Yes, thank you,' he replied cautiously.

'I'll ask Hazel to bring some ginger pop and gummy bears and you can tell me all about it.' Lorelli smiled.

'Tell you about what?'

Lorelli sighed. 'Why can't we trust each other?'

'Force of habit, I suppose.'

'It's Felicia,' said Lorelli.

'What is?' Ovid tried to hide his embarrassment.

'She's the one trying to kill me. She cut the chandelier and gave me the statue and this morning she locked me in her parents' studio and cut the power so that the glass would explode.'

'The chandelier, the statue and the exploding vases,' said Ovid. 'All glass. If she is trying to kill you, she's certainly got style.'

'This isn't a joke.'

'Of course it's a joke. Felicia? A murderer? She's harmless. Anyway, she can't have tried to kill you this morning.'

'Oh, this was after your little encounter with her by the old mill.'

'You've been spying on me,' said Ovid.

Lorelli looked pityingly at her brother. 'We need to look out for each other,' she said. 'We need to be honest with each other.'

'I don't think that's possible for us,' said Ovid. 'But I don't think you're right about Felicia. It was Dragos who lied to us and I just saw him walking up towards the mine.'

'Dragos has been nothing but good to us since his arrival,' said Lorelli.

'So you trust him, do you?' replied Ovid.

'What are you saying? That he was behind the attacks? For what reason?'

'Maybe there is something about Old Silas's mine.'

The twins' conversation was interrupted by the sound of an approaching motor. Ovid turned around to see a police car pulling up outside. 'Don't say you called the police,' he said.

'No,' said Lorelli.

The car stopped and Sergeant Putnam squeezed himself out of the driver's seat.

'Afternoon, young Thornthwaites.' The large police officer took out his notepad and flicked it open. 'Now, I think you probably know why I'm here.'

'Actually no,' said Ovid.

Sergeant Putnam coughed. 'A rather serious matter of a fugitive you are harbouring on your estate.'

Lorelli and Ovid looked at each other, both thinking the same thing. Jenny. Uncle Harry had warned them the authorities would come looking for her.

'We have no idea what you're talking about,' said Lorelli.

'Now, now,' Sergeant Putnam shook his head. 'Lying to an officer of the law is not a good idea. I have reliable witnesses that she was seen coming here. Let's not make this more difficult than it needs to be.'

'We promised our uncle we would look after her until he's back,' said Ovid.

'Your uncle? What's your uncle got to do with anything?' asked Sergeant Putnam.

'He's the one who brought her here,' said Ovid.

'Did he indeed? Then maybe I should speak to him.'

'He only did it to save her,' said Lorelli. 'He says she won't survive in the wild.'

'In the wild?'

'Africa or wherever they take her to release her.'

'Why would they take Mrs Bagshaw to Africa?'

'Mrs Bagshaw?' said the twins.

Escape From
the Manor

As soon as Hazel saw the police car pull up outside, she knew why it was there. Mrs Bagshaw had not been let out of prison because of her soup. She had escaped. Hazel ran to the kitchen immediately and found her peeling potatoes.

'Hello, Hazel, my love. Grab a peeler, would you? I'm making my industrial pie. You know, the one that's like cottage pie only much bigger. I'm going to need a lot of spuds.'

'Mum, you have to go. Sergeant Putnam is here.'

'Not to worry, dear. There's plenty for everyone.' Mrs Bagshaw sped up her peeling. 'Although you're right – he does have a big appetite. Yes, we'll definitely need more spuds. Come on now, roll up your sleeves and lend a hand.'

'Mum, stop.' Hazel grabbed her wrist. Mrs Bagshaw was gripping the peeler so tightly her knuckles were white. There was nothing left of the potato, and the blade of the peeler had nipped the palm of her hand. A drop of blood fell into the pan of water.

'Look what you've made me do now,' said Mrs Bagshaw. 'We'd better wash those.'

'We have to go,' said Hazel. 'He'll take you back.'

'Back?' A look of horror crossed Mrs Bagshaw's face. 'I don't want to go back, Hazel. You won't let him take me back there, will you? It's an awful place. I'd much rather not go back.'

'Then you need to come with me now.'

Mrs Bagshaw dropped the peeler and grabbed her coat.

'No. No coat,' said Hazel.

'Now, I know it's warm in the sun today but it's chilly in the shade. I'm not going out without a coat. On the run or not.'

'They'll be looking for that one,' said Hazel. 'I will find you something else.'

They stepped out of the back door, then Hazel walked briskly around the rose bushes with Mrs Bagshaw behind her, trying to keep up. When they reached the driveway, Hazel paused to check no one was around before dashing to the stables. Mrs Bagshaw waited behind a bush until Hazel returned with one of Tom's black riding jackets.

'I'm not putting that on,' said Mrs Bagshaw. 'It's filthy.'

'Please,' said Hazel.

Hazel could see the conflict in her mum's eyes. She couldn't tell if she was more scared of being caught or of admitting that she was scared. Mrs Bagshaw had always put on a brave face by avoiding the truth. It was all she knew.

'They'll be looking for you,' said Hazel. 'Please. For me.'

Mrs Bagshaw embraced her briefly, then put the jacket on. 'It will do for now,' she said. 'Let's be off.'

Hazel led her through the woods, down to the main road. On the way, Mrs Bagshaw complained a lot about her legs, but Hazel kept her moving. At the road, they waited for ten minutes before a bus turned up. Hazel flagged it down and they got on.

'Why, if it ain't Hilda Bagshaw,' said the driver.

She stared at him blankly.

'Dickie,' said the bus driver. 'Surely you remember me.'

'Oh yes, hello,' said Mrs Bagshaw.

'Back working at the manor, are you?' said the driver.

'Please can we get moving?' Hazel glanced anxiously over her shoulder.

'What's that?' said Dickie.

'The bus,' said Hazel. 'Please can we get moving? We're in a hurry.'

Dickie closed the door and set off. 'I can only go as fast as the timetable allows,' he said.

Hazel was grateful they were the only ones on the bus, but she kept glancing behind her, looking for the police car.

'I say, do you still make that bread and butter pudding?' asked Dickie.

Mrs Bagshaw smiled for the first time since they'd left the kitchen. 'I haven't changed my recipe in twenty-five years. How do you know about that then?'

'You made it for Lord and Lady Thornthwaite's wedding all them years ago, but I can still remember it.'

Mrs Bagshaw giggled. 'Oh, you always were a charmer. Yes, I made it for Lord and Lady Thornthwaite's wedding breakfast.'

'I remember it like it were yesterday. I was eating it when we were called on to remove Lady Thornthwaite's brother.'

Hazel wasn't listening. A car was approaching. Even in the distance, she could see that it was Sergeant Putnam's police car. 'Mum, get down,' she said.

'What's that?' asked Mrs Bagshaw.

'Duck.' Hazel had no choice but to push Mrs Bagshaw's head down just in time to hide her from view as the police car overtook.

'You two all right back there?' said Dickie.

'Fine, thank you,' said Hazel. 'I dropped something but I've found it now.'

'And where are you two off on this fine day?'

'The train station,' said Hazel.

'Off on a day trip, is it?' asked Dickie.

'Yes,' said Mrs Bagshaw. 'It's just nice to get away from it all sometimes, isn't it?'

A Traditional
Family Stew

The twins sat at the dining table in the room with one wall. Dragos had hung tarpaulin around the missing walls. It flapped noisily. A naked bulb hung over them where the chandelier had been. Ovid looked up at it. It flickered, buzzed and swung in the breeze. 'So Mrs Bagshaw is on the run, Hazel's gone with her, Beaufort's left, Uncle Harry is still in hospital and I haven't seen Nurse Griddle or Tom since this morning.'

'What's your point?' asked Lorelli.

'Who's going to cook dinner?' said Ovid.

'That's what you're worried about?'

'It is when I'm hungry,' said Ovid. 'I'll find Nurse Griddle.'

'This is our problem,' Lorelli stated angrily. 'We rely on everyone else. We shouldn't have servants running around after us. We need to be able to look after ourselves.'

'Running around? We've got two left and they're hardly ever here. I've never seen them run.'

'Two is more servants than most children have. This life isn't normal.'

Ovid smirked. 'Is that what you want to be? Normal?'

'What's wrong with wanting to be normal?'

'It's unrealistic for us.'

'How many times do we need to almost die before you believe that Felicia is trying to kill me?'

'A couple more times, I think.'

'Do you know what I think?'

'No. Do tell me, my dear sister.'

'I think she wants you to help her get rid of me.'

Ovid laughed. 'Oh come on. I suppose she's waiting behind that door, ready to step out, reveal her evil plot and then murder us.'

Dragos pushed aside a roll of tarpaulin and stepped into the room, holding a tray with a large bowl. He placed it down on the table.

'You are growing children. You must eat,' he announced.

'What is it?' Ovid lent over to smell the dish.

'Traditional Romanian meal. Kind of stew.' Dragos lifted off the lid and used a ladle to serve out two portions into bowls, which he placed in front of the twins.

'This is very kind of you,' said Lorelli.

'The old lady's children are my family. Now, eat. It is an old family recipe. I will be insulted if the bowl is not licked clean.'

Ovid handed Lorelli a spoon.

'You first,' he said.

'Certainly,' she replied, taking the spoon and trying it.

'It is tasty, yes?' said Dragos, pouring himself a bowl and tucking in.

'It's delicious,' said Lorelli.

Ovid tasted it. It was good. 'How come everyone in this house is a better cook than our actual cook?' he asked.

'Just the right amount of salt, yes?' said Dragos. 'On his deathbed, my father's final words were, *Dragos, don't forget the salt.*'

'This is the father who worked for our grandfather, is it?' asked Ovid.

Dragos blew on his spoon to cool the stew. 'You know about that?'

'Yes,' said Ovid. 'Tom told us your father was a miner. I saw you walking up there earlier on. What were you looking for?'

'Only to make it safe. My father was no miner. He was gold prospector. At least, that is what he called himself. He was the one who suggested Silas dig a mine in the first place.'

'A prospector? But I thought no gold was found,' said Lorelli.

'This is true, but to his dying day my father believed that there was gold down there. *Dragos, the old lady lies on top of a great fortune,* he would say. This is what Tom wanted to stop you from learning. He feared you would think that was why I came here.'

'Is that why you came here?' said Ovid. 'Are you here to find your father's gold?'

'No. My father was not a good prospector. He was not good at much of anything. Except this stew. He never found any gold his whole life. All that mine contains is danger and death.'

'Why did you come here if not for the gold?' asked Ovid.

'I have told you many times the reason. The old lady called out to me. I am here to nurse her back to health. Now, finish your stew or you will cause great offence to my family.'

Everything
Except Murder

Sitting in her room rereading Alfred Crutcher's book, Lorelli wondered if Uncle Harry was right about these stories being too dark for children. Strangely, it had never been the stories of death and murder that worried her. It was the repeated failure of her ancestors. No Lord Thornthwaite ever lived to reach his potential. In the eighteenth century, Allegro had a passion for music, but his symphonies died with him after his wife laced their pages with deadly poison. In the nineteenth century, Lord Christof's dreams of being a great architect crumbled and he threw himself off the top of his own wonky tower. In the twentieth century, their grandfather loved gold so much he invested in a mine that brought nothing but death. Generation after generation, Thornthwaites had failed at everything they tried.

Everything except murder.

She shut the book and lay back on the bed with her hands behind her head. She closed her eyes and brought to mind Beaufort's meal. The memory of its flavours lingered on her tongue. The interruption of Uncle Harry's heart attack

223

had left her with a feeling of unease, as though she had been reading a novel only to find the final few pages torn out. She thought about trying to write about the Russian dressmaker, but all she could see in her mind's eye were the oppressive corridors of Thornthwaite Manor. She reached for her copy of *The Seven Dances of Franciska T'oth*. She didn't need to open the book. She knew every word. It was a comfort simply to hold it. Franciska's life was tragic, but it was perfect in its tragedy.

Lorelli rolled off the bed and went to the window, where she looked out at the darkening sky. She could see Dragos's outline on the sloping tower as he made the most of the last rays of the daylight.

She imagined Lord Christof climbing up and leaping off. The towers looked like devil horns against the night sky. Lorelli caught her own reflection in the window. She saw her face imprinted on the imposing backdrop. Staring into her own eyes, she understood with absolute certainty what she had to do.

Dragos worried that the old lady was dying, but the truth was that Lorelli and Ovid had been moving around inside a corpse since birth. Thornthwaite Manor was a prison. It was a dead weight. It was a death trap.

Beaufort's story needed an ending and Lorelli understood what that was now. Escape. Lorelli had to leave the only place she had ever known. It was the only way to break out of her old self and be the person she wanted to be. It was the only hope she had of ever being normal.

It was time to start afresh.

Escape by Train

Hazel had no previous experience of helping a wanted criminal evade the law, but she knew they had to move quickly. The train station was the next place Sergeant Putnam would check. She told Mrs Bagshaw to hide in a phone box while she bought two train tickets, then they stepped out onto the platform. There was only one other person waiting for the train. A man stood with a tattered suitcase and a small bowler hat.

He turned to look at them and spoke.

''Azel,' said Beaufort. 'You are 'ere to beg me not to go, but I made a promise to your mother.'

'I am her mother,' said Mrs Bagshaw.

'I was talking about 'er other mother,' said Beaufort.

'Who are you?' she asked.

'Apparently that is a matter of opinion,' he replied.

'This is my father,' said Hazel.

'This is Artie Newly?' Mrs Bagshaw scrutinised him intently. 'Oh yes, there is a resemblance now you mention it. Well I never. Artie Newly.'

'You need to help us,' said Hazel. 'We can't let them catch my mum.'

'You are on the run?' said Beaufort.

'I am no such thing,' said Mrs Bagshaw. 'There's just been a bit of a misunderstanding. That's all. Suffice it to say, turnips.'

'Turnips?'

'Please,' said Hazel. 'She needs your help. I need your help.'

'It is impossible.'

'But you've done it before,' said Hazel. 'You've changed who you are. You can help us get away.'

'That is different. I was not on the run. No, I cannot,' protested Beaufort.

'Please. For me,' begged Hazel.

An automatic announcement said, *'The next train on platform one will arrive in two minutes . . .'*

'This is why I ran away in the first place,' said Beaufort. 'I realise I am a selfish man. I have made my peace with that. I sacrificed life for the sake of my art, but since finding you, 'Azel, I 'ave been overcome with a most alarming and unnatural feeling. It is as though none of it matters.'

'None of what matters?' said Mrs Bagshaw. 'What's he talking about?'

Beaufort did not shift his gaze from Hazel. 'All of my creations are nothing compared to my most magnificent creation. You, 'Azel. I am talking about you. The true burden of parenthood is the understanding that our children are worth all sacrifices. I tried to avoid that truth, but fate brought us together and now I feel a pitiful compulsion to 'elp you.'

Hazel threw her arms around Beaufort. Beaufort embraced her.

'*The train is now approaching platform one*,' said the automated voice. '*Please stand away from the edge of the platform.*'

'You'll help us hide?' said Hazel.

'No,' said Beaufort. 'I will help Mrs Bagshaw hide. You must remain at Thornthwaite Manor.'

'What? But no. I must come with you . . . with her. You can't leave me behind.'

Beaufort took Hazel's hands in his. 'That is the biggest and most painful sacrifice I must make. We cannot take you with us.'

'Why?' Hazel could hear the clattering of the approaching train as though it was rattling through the arteries of her heart.

'I promised Eileen,' said Beaufort. 'I promised I would not take you away.'

'But . . .'

'He's right, dear,' said Mrs Bagshaw. 'Nurse Griddle would fall to pieces if you disappeared. You must stay and look after her, my dear girl. You must look after each other. Don't burn bridges because of my silly mistakes.'

The train's brakes squealed as it came to a standstill. Hazel felt a tear roll down her cheek. 'But Nurse Griddle is so cold.'

'Then you must warm 'er up, 'Azel.'

Mrs Bagshaw wiped the tear away. 'She does love you in her own way. She just isn't sure how to show it. You need to teach her, my dear girl, and I believe you can.'

'It is the only way, 'Azel.'

Beaufort opened the train door and placed his suitcase inside. He held out a hand for Mrs Bagshaw, but Hazel was clinging onto her. Her hugs had been the thing she had missed most while she was away, because they had always made her feel safe.

'I want to go with you,' she sobbed.

'My dear girl . . .' Mrs Bagshaw released her and held her firmly by the shoulders. 'I wish I could take you, but you would have to spend your life in hiding. You deserve more than that.'

'We must leave,' said Beaufort. ''Azel, I'm sorry.' He took Mrs Bagshaw's hand and helped her onto the train.

'I want to create art like you do,' sobbed Hazel.

Beaufort smiled. 'I 'ave only ever created fleeting sensations. You must create something that lasts longer with your mother. She needs you more than you realise.'

'*The train at platform one is now ready to depart,*' said the automatic announcement.

'Will I see you again?' said Hazel.

'When it is safe, I will send for you,' said Beaufort. 'Until then, please understand, I do this out of love. Do you understand?'

Through her tears, Hazel could only manage two words. '*Oui*, chef.'

Beaufort shut the door and the train pulled away.

A New Game

Lorelli was jolted awake by a loud noise. In her confused half-asleep state it had sounded like an explosion, but she ran to the window and saw that Ovid was on the croquet pitch, lining up his mallet. He took aim and whacked the ball. The sound echoed off the walls, startling a flock of birds resting in a nearby tree. Lorelli quickly dressed and went down to join him.

As she stepped out onto the lawn, Ovid was lining up another shot. 'What *are* you doing?'

'Playing croquet. What does it look like? Do you want to join me or would that not be normal enough for you?'

'I don't think it's normal to play anything at this time in the morning, but seeing as we're up I suppose I may as well.'

Ovid hit the ball but it bounced off the side of the hoop. 'It's harder than it looks.'

'Let me see.' Lorelli took the mallet from his hands and got into position. 'I've made a decision.'

'About what?'

'I'm leaving.'

'You're going out?'

'No. I'm leaving Thornthwaite Manor.'

'Very funny.'

'I'm not joking.'

'Where would you go?' asked Ovid.

'I don't know yet.'

'But this is our home.'

'Is it?' Lorelli made the shot. The ball went straight through the hoop.

'You think by leaving you can escape who we are?' Ovid snatched the mallet off her.

'I want to try.'

Ovid picked up the ball. He tossed it and caught it in the same hand. It came naturally to him to argue with his sister, but ever since Beaufort's story meal he had felt the same. For centuries, Lord and Lady Thornthwaites had lived up to the terrible legacy of their family name. The twins didn't just owe it to themselves to get out. They owed it to their ancestors.

'Yes,' he said quietly.

'Yes, what?' said Lorelli.

'Yes, let's sell and go.'

'Sell Thornthwaite Manor?' said Lorelli. 'We don't have to sell, just move out.'

'It's the only way,' said Ovid. 'We need to leave, and leave properly.'

'We're not allowed to sell until we turn sixteen,' said Lorelli. 'Before then, it's Tom and Nurse Griddle's decision.'

'Uncle Harry will find a way,' said Ovid. 'He has a whole team of lawyers who will be able to make it happen.'

'Then we're agreed,' said Lorelli. 'A fresh start.'

Ovid made another shot but chipped it and sent it flying off at an angle. They looked to see where it landed and Old Tom stepped out from behind a rose bush. He held the croquet ball in one hand and a fistful of plants in the other. 'Morning, young masters.'

'Were you eavesdropping, Tom?' demanded Ovid.

'Only a bit,' replied the ancient gardener casually. 'I came to look for you when I noticed a few weeds that needed pulling up. So you've decided to sell the manor then?'

'I suppose you're going to try to stop us, are you?' said Lorelli.

'It's not my place to stop you doing anything, and young Master Ovid is right: your uncle has enough lawyers to make it happen even if Nurse Griddle and I try to stop you.'

'But surely you want us to stay,' said Ovid.

Tom rolled the ball back to him. 'Of course.'

Ovid stopped it with his foot.

'That's it? That's all you've got to say?' said Lorelli.

'You've made up your minds, and in my experience trying to persuade folk against what they've decided to do is like trying to stop a tree growing with a pair of secateurs. No matter how much pruning you do, the tree will grow. The only way to stop a tree growing is to chop it down altogether.'

'So you won't try to stop us?' Lorelli had been expecting more of a fight.

'If you're sure it's what you want,' said Tom. 'All I'll say is that it will be a shame if all this is lost.'

'The house is basically a ruin anyway,' said Lorelli.

231

'I'm not talking about Thornthwaite Manor. It's made of stone and bricks, no matter what Dragos would have you believe. The estate, on the other hand, is Mother Nature's handiwork and it has remained unspoiled all these years because it's been under the protection of your family. You sell up and they'll build some godawful superstore faster than it takes one of my bees to pollinate the raspberries.'

'Then we'll make sure it's sold to someone who will keep it as it is. Uncle Harry will help us,' said Lorelli.

'It seems Uncle Harry is the solution to all of your problems,' said Tom. 'So it's good that he is currently sitting in the drawing room waiting to see you.'

'He's out of hospital?' said Ovid.

'He is indeed, and now that I've informed you I have some business with a trowel and a field of potatoes. Good day, young masters.'

Leopard on the Loose

Before the great fire struck, the drawing room had held portraits of previous generations of Thornthwaites. Now, the walls were bare and the only piece of furniture was the blackened chaise longue where Uncle Harry was sitting sipping a cup of coffee.

'Should you be drinking that in your condition?' asked Lorelli.

He took a sip. 'I am enjoying it, which means probably not. But I'm done with being told not to do things. My time is limited. I intend to spend what I have making things right.'

'Good. Then help us sell the estate,' said Lorelli.

'Sell?' said Uncle Harry.

'Yes. We've decided to leave this place behind,' said Lorelli.

'Really? That's a big decision. Where did this come from?'

'It's time to go,' said Ovid.

Uncle Harry placed his mug on the back of the chaise longue. 'I can't tell you how relieved I am to hear you say that. It would be my honour to help you move on.'

'Thank you.' Lorelli picked up the mug and placed it on a windowsill.

'Have you informed your servants yet?'

'We just told Tom. He understands,' said Ovid.

'Even if he wanted to stop you, it wouldn't be a problem. You are the rightful heirs. Everything else can be dealt with.'

Uncle Harry stood up but was still feeling weak and would have fallen back down had Lorelli and Ovid not each taken a hand to steady him. They were holding him up when Dragos entered the room.

'Lorelli, Ovid . . .' he said urgently, 'you must get to your rooms now. We have problem.'

'What problem?' asked Uncle Harry.

Dragos scowled at him. 'Leopard problem,' he said.

'Jenny is safe enough down in that mine.' Harry released his niece and nephew.

'She is not down in mine any more. After I spoke to Lorelli and Ovid I realised I must shut it down. It is too dangerous. This morning I used explosives to collapse the shaft.'

'So I didn't dream that explosion—' began Lorelli.

'If you've harmed her –' interrupted Harry.

'Do not worry. I removed your leopard first,' said Dragos.

'Removed her where?' asked Lorelli.

'I tied her to a post. Very safely. Except the explosion must have shaken post. This Jenny is on the loose. I do not know where.'

'You've lost her?' said Uncle Harry.

'You should not bring wild animals to this place. They are not safe. I will go find Old Tom's guns.'

'I forbid you to shoot my leopard!' exclaimed Uncle Harry.

Dragos puffed out his chest and took a step closer. 'You are a foolish man. I will use tranquilliser and make safe. In meantime, I insist that *you* stay safe. Remain in the house.' Dragos left.

'A leopard on the loose.' Ovid turned to Lorelli. 'Something told me it was going to be one of those mornings,' he added wryly.

'When did she last eat?' asked Uncle Harry.

'It was the wildebeest,' said Lorelli.

'That was two days ago. She'll be starving.'

'So, what? The kitchen?' said Ovid.

'Or the livestock,' said Uncle Harry.

'The horses!' exclaimed Lorelli.

Fresh Meat in a
Pink Dress

Ovid followed his sister as she ran from the drawing room out through the front door to the stables. Uncle Harry was unable to keep up, so it was just the two of them. As they approached, they heard the leopard's growl, the horses' whinnies and a girl's scream from within Joy's stable. Lorelli opened the door to find Felicia in a pretty pink dress cowering in front of the leopard. Joy was behind a rickety door, rearing up, snorting and stamping her feet. Jenny, the leopard, was crouching down, ready to pounce.

'Oh, Ovvy-wovvy, help me,' pleaded Felicia. 'I don't want to die.'

Since the incident at the glassworks, in her mind Lorelli had transformed Felicia into a two-faced murderous monster. Seeing her now, cowering and crying, she looked totally pathetic.

'Felicia? What are you doing here?' asked Lorelli.

'I came to see you and Ovvy—' she began.

The leopard growled.

She continued in a whisper. '—wovvy. I passed the stables

and thought it would be nice to feed a sugar lump to the horses, then this happened.'

'Shoo,' said Ovid. 'Jenny, back down.'

For a moment it seemed as though the leopard was considering it, but Felicia whimpered, reminding Jenny about the fresh meat, nicely wrapped in a pink dress.

'I don't think that worked,' said Lorelli.

'Worth a try though,' said Ovid.

'Please,' begged Felicia. 'Help me.'

'We need something to coax her away,' said Ovid. 'Lorelli, go to the kitchen and find some meat. I'll try to keep her distracted until you get back.'

'Don't worry, Felicia,' said Lorelli. 'Just think of her as a big pussycat. Ovid, don't let anything happen to that horse.'

'The horse!' exclaimed Felicia. 'What about me?'

'Or Felicia,' added Lorelli before running out.

'Oh, Ovvy, do you think this is where it will end for us?' whimpered Felicia. 'Mauled to death by a wild animal while you are forced to watch, helpless to save me. How tragically romantic.'

'Felicia,' said Ovid, 'there is nothing romantic about being killed by a leopard, but you will be all right if you stay still and keep quiet.'

'Sorry, Ovvy-wovvy. It's just that since we . . .'

Jenny stepped forward, silencing Felicia. She sniffed at her imminent meal. Felicia screamed. The leopard snarled. Joy neighed and kicked up her legs. They connected with the stable door and sent it flying off its hinges, knocking Felicia to the ground. With the door broken, Joy was free to make her escape. She jumped over the broken door and bolted out of the stable. Jenny was confused for a moment, until she noticed that the fresh meat in the pink dress was lying still. The leopard lowered its head to feast on its meal.

'Jenny, Jenny, Jenny!' Ovid waved his arms around and jumped up and down.

Jenny turned to look at this new creature dressed in black. Not as tender as the pink dress, but still perfectly edible.

'Now go,' muttered Ovid. 'Quickly.'

'Oh, Ovvy-wovvy,' whispered Felicia as she slipped out of the stable. The leopard didn't notice. It had a new prey in its sights. Ovid took a step back. Jenny matched him with a step closer. He bent his knees. Jenny crouched down. He maintained eye contact. He tried to hide his fear. Animals could smell fear. That much he knew. Ovid knew he had been in worse predicaments. He just couldn't bring them to mind right now.

A Purr and a Growl

As far as Ovid was aware, no other previous Lord Thornthwaite had ever been killed and eaten by a leopard. Staring into Jenny's hungry eyes, he tried to console himself with the thought that his would be an original death, but it was no real consolation. The possibility of dying was a harsh reminder that he had not yet lived. Kissing Felicia had been an uncomfortable and worrying experience, but it had made him realise there was more to life.

'Now, Jenny –' Ovid addressed the growling leopard directly – 'in a minute my sister is going to come back with a lovely bit of wildebeest. Yum, wildebeest. Or elk. Or . . . look, I don't know what she's coming back with, but whatever it is I promise you it will taste nicer than me.'

The leopard's leg muscles tightened as she prepared to pounce. There was nothing else Ovid could do. He had been backed into a corner. He closed his eyes and waited.

If this was how it ended, then let it end. At least it would be over. Having spent his life in the shadow of death, there should at least be some comfort when it came for him, even if it came in the shape of a ravenous wild animal.

Ovid heard the growl.

Then a purr.

He opened his eyes and saw Cowell jumping down from a beam. The cat landed in front of him. He looked at the leopard, but Jenny was staring at Cowell.

The cat's hair stood on end. She arched her back and hissed. Ovid could see her claws. Cowell was trying to look as threatening as possible. Jenny did the same with considerably more success. Both cats stood face to face, whiskers twitching, baring their teeth, claws at the ready. Cowell meowed. Jenny growled.

Ovid edged to the side, keeping his eyes on the leopard. He moved as slowly and quietly as possible, watching the two cats staring at each other, neither daring to make a move, neither daring to look away. Ovid's route out of the stables took him within claws' reach of Jenny. She caught his scent and turned to look at him.

Ovid had his back to the wall. There was no possibility of escape. If Jenny pounced now, he would be reduced to mincemeat in seconds. Cowell must have understood this too, because she jumped up and sank her claws into Jenny's hide. The leopard casually batted her away. Cowell screeched and let go.

Jenny turned back to Ovid and he knew this was the moment. There was no point in coming up with clever quips or pithy puns. He was about to be mauled to death by a leopard. It was a brutal way to go, but it wasn't the pain that worried him. It was the finality.

'Din-dins, Jenny!' called a voice.

Ovid turned to see Lorelli standing in the doorway. For

a moment, he wondered if this was all part of one of her tricks. Had she set the whole thing up? Was she about to get the last laugh as she finally got the better of him?

Thankfully not.

Lorelli winked, then threw a huge slab of meat towards the leopard and Jenny dived onto it and sank her teeth into the flesh. Ovid snatched up Cowell in his arms and ran.

Tomorrow's Steak

Lorelli shut the stable door and Ovid patted Cowell's head.

'Thanks for your help,' he said.

Cowell meowed.

Ovid tickled her under the chin, then put her down gently. She rubbed herself against his leg and he scratched her side.

'She must be running out of lives by now,' said Lorelli.

'So must we,' replied Ovid. 'Where's Felicia?'

'She went straight past me. Judging by what she was screaming, I don't think she'll be coming back soon.'

'So I guess that takes her off the list of suspects,' said Ovid.

'Yes. You were right. She's just a silly girl.'

Dragos appeared around the corner. Under one arm he held a shotgun. 'The leopard is in there?' he said.

'Yes. Don't hurt her,' said Lorelli.

'Tranquillisers.' Dragos tapped the barrel of the gun. 'I will put her to sleep. It is not safe having wild animal on the loose. Now, please, go somewhere safe.'

'Where's safe in Thornthwaite manor?' said Ovid.

'The old lady might have secrets, but the only dangers she contains are flesh and blood,' said Dragos.

'What does that mean?' said Lorelli.

'It means just that people do bad things. Buildings do not.' With a tip of his cap, Dragos opened the stable door and stepped inside.

Neither twin wanted to hear Jenny being shot, so they walked briskly towards the house.

'Another day, another near-death experience,' said Ovid.

'But who's behind it?' asked Lorelli.

Her question went unanswered as the twins heard a scream from the kitchen.

'Felicia?' said Lorelli.

'Hazel,' said Ovid.

They broke into a run. There was a second scream, but this one was muffled under the sound of their breathing and the crunch of the gravel beneath their shoes. Ovid flung open the door and they both stepped inside just as a pair of knives flew at their heads. It was not the first time they had avoided flying knives. They ducked and the knives missed.

Millicent Hartwell stood behind the kitchen counter. She selected a fresh knife from the wooden block. Felicia lay flat on the counter while Hazel was huddled on the kitchen floor, nursing a bleeding arm.

'Hazel, are you all right?' asked Ovid.

'Yes, sir. In pain, sir.'

'Millicent, what have you done?' said Lorelli.

'Nothing,' she replied. 'Nothing yet. Felicia fainted when she saw the knife and Hazel got in my way.' She picked up a sharpening tool and dragged the knife along the steel.

'Maybe you should put the knives down,' said Ovid.

'*Maybe you should put the knives down,*' mocked Millicent. 'And maybe I shouldn't.'

'Why are you doing this?' said Lorelli. 'Ovid doesn't even like Felicia, do you, Ovid?'

'I can honestly say I do not like her,' said Ovid. 'Hand on heart.'

'What heart?' Millicent flung a bread knife. Ovid dodged. It hit a cabinet and clattered to the ground. 'I saw you kissing her,' spat Millicent.

'She was kissing me,' said Ovid.

'Do not lie.' Millicent brought the knife down so close to Felicia's fingers that one of her false nails went pinging off. 'You were kissing her. You saw it too, Lorelli.'

'I did, but like I said, my brother is an idiot.'

'Thanks,' said Ovid.

'Idiot or not, he betrayed me,' said Millicent.

'It wasn't me that broke it off,' protested Ovid. 'Your dad said I couldn't see you.'

'And so you gave up,' said Millicent. 'You weren't supposed to give up. Didn't your silly research tell you anything?'

'You told her about the research?' Ovid said to Lorelli.

'I was trying to make her feel better after you'd been kissing Felicia.'

Ovid was confused. 'So Mr Hartwell's warnings were supposed to make me like Millicent more?'

'Forbidden love and all that,' said Lorelli.

'Exactly,' Millicent whispered. 'But instead, you ran straight off into Felicia's arms.'

'That's not fair,' protested Ovid. 'I thought I was meeting you.'

Another flying knife missed his head by a millimetre and lodged itself in the wall behind.

Millicent drew another. 'We could have been such a good team. With your sister gone we would have been happy,' she said.

'I'm sorry? Gone?' said Lorelli.

'Oh, come on. I loosened the chandelier. I positioned the statue,' said Millicent. 'It took me ages to work out the exact place to catch the first sunlight. Cutting off the electricity at the glassworks would have been messier but still as effective.'

'It was you? You've been trying to kill us?' said Lorelli.

'Just you.' Millicent spat on the floor and brought a blade down again, cutting off a tuft of Felicia's hair. She lifted it up and sniffed it. 'Oh my, it smells of strawberries and cream and wonderful things. I wonder whether the rest of her will smell so nice when I chop her up.'

'Millicent, you don't need to do this,' said Ovid. 'I don't even like Felicia. I like you.'

'Me?'

'Yes.'

'So prove it and help me kill her, then we'll dispose of your sister and your mousy maid.'

Ovid took a step towards her. 'You want me to kill Felicia, Lorelli and Hazel?'

Millicent waved the knife at him. 'You're Ovid Thornthwaite, aren't you? Killing is in your blood. It'll be easy. Today's wounded are tomorrow's steak.'

'You're right,' said Ovid. 'I'll help. Give me a knife.' He took another step, but Millicent swiped the blade to keep him back.

'You think I would trust you after what you did?' said Millicent. 'I'll never trust you.'

Living in Denial

Hazel lay on the floor, bleeding. Pain muddied her thoughts. She saw Ovid and Lorelli enter. She saw the blades fly. She heard Ovid ask her a question. She responded automatically but she couldn't hold onto what was said. The effort of talking made her dizzy and sick. Her mind drifted as she felt the cold comfort of the kitchen tiles. Millicent was standing over Felicia. The twins were too far away to stop her.

'So all that stuff you told me about Felicia wanting our money, that was you all along?' said Lorelli.

'It's not about money,' said Millicent. 'I want it all.'

'What does that mean?' asked Lorelli. 'The estate? The manor?'

'The name,' said Millicent. 'I want to be a Thornthwaite.'

'Why?' asked Lorelli. 'You know what we are.'

'Yes,' said Millicent. 'You aren't afraid. You'll stop at nothing. I don't want to take your lives. I want to *have* your lives. Thornthwaites don't think twice about killing. I can be like that too.'

'What are you talking about?' said Ovid. 'We've never killed anyone. I mean, we've tried, but neither of us has ever succeeded.'

'I know. You're both weak. You haven't the guts to finish the job. I would have been a better Thornthwaite than either of you,' said Millicent.

'What are you talking about? You're not a Thornthwaite,' said Ovid.

She looked at him pityingly. 'I could have been,' she said. 'I should have been.'

'Millicent, this is crazy,' said Lorelli. 'I mean, actually properly crazy.'

'You can say that again,' said Ovid.

Millicent dropped her knife and tapped her head. 'Don't call me that,' she snarled. 'I'm not crazy. I'm not. I have ideas. I make up stories, like everyone does. Don't call me crazy. Doctor Mingus says it's my trigger word.'

'Doctor Mingus.' Lorelli recognised the name at once. 'But . . . that's Adam's doctor. How do you . . . ? You see the same specialist as Adam?' Lorelli recalled his letters. She remembered the girl he sometimes mentioned. 'You're the truth partner, the one he talks about from group. That's you, isn't it?'

'Yes, but I'm not going to those sessions any more. Dad thought I was confused about the difference between truth and lies, but it's him who is confused about everything. He's living in denial.'

'Millicent, did you tell Father Whelan that your father killed your mother?' asked Lorelli.

'He must have.' Millicent wiped her brow with a sleeve, then picked up the knife again. 'She would never have left me.'

'You're not well,' said Lorelli. 'You need help.'

Every word Millicent spoke brought the strength back to Hazel's limbs and pushed the pain further into the background. She had to stop her. Adrenaline rushed through her body. She saw things clearly. The hysterical girl with the knife. The twins unable to get near enough to stop her. The large halibut lying on the floor with one dead eye staring at her. Hazel hated those fish eyes. They goaded her.

She had always been a good servant, as useful and unremarkable as a familiar piece of furniture. Invisible. A minor character in someone else's story. Now, she saw clearly that she could make a difference. She reached for the halibut. It was slippery but she got a firm grip. Millicent didn't notice.

In one sudden, painful move, Hazel jumped up and brought the fish onto the side of Millicent's head. The knives clattered to the ground and Millicent's head caught the edge of the kitchen counter. Hazel watched her crumple to the ground. She had a moment to enjoy her triumph before joining her on the floor.

A Slight Gesture

Hazel awoke to the rare vision of daylight around the edges of the curtains. Her first thought was that she had overslept, but slowly the memory of the horror in the kitchen came back to her.

'What's happening?' She sat upright suddenly.

'Relax, you're safe now. The danger has gone.' Nurse Griddle was sitting beside her bed, providing Hazel with an alarming up-nostril view of her over-sized nose.

'But Ovid, Lorelli . . . and Felicia. They're . . .'

'They are all well.'

'Where's Millicent?'

'Somewhere she will be looked after. I gather that she is a very disturbed young lady.'

'And Felicia?'

'Back with her parents.'

'So everything is back to normal?'

Nurse Griddle drew the curtains and picked up a vase of flowers from the bedside table. 'Not entirely. The twins are leaving Thornthwaite Manor. They are going to sell the estate.'

'Sell the estate?'

'Yes. They are quite adamant. Nothing Tom or I have said can dissuade them, and Mr Marshall has a team of lawyers that can get around our guardianship.'

'What will happen to us?'

'We will be looked after. We're all being offered generous pensions – Tom, Mrs Bagshaw and me. You will not want for anything. Dragos is upset of course, but he respects the twins' reasons and they have allowed him to continue working on the house until it is sold.'

'Why do they want to sell?'

'They want to move on with their lives.'

Hazel looked up at the ceiling. Thornthwaite Manor had been all she had ever known. She could not imagine anything else. 'Where will we live?'

'I was thinking we could move to the village. Just the two of us. Then, when you're old enough, you could go to catering college. Or whatever you want. Hazel, I want to do right by you.'

Nurse Griddle squeezed Hazel's hand. It was the kind of slight gesture most people would have done unthinkingly, but this was Nurse Griddle. Hazel understood the significance of that hand squeeze. It was the equivalent to one of Mrs Bagshaw's biggest hugs. It was a slight gesture that meant so much. She could tell Nurse Griddle was embarrassed, but she left her hand there anyway.

'What a week it has been,' said Nurse Griddle. 'Explosions, floods, fires, psychopathic butchers' daughters and . . .'

'And my father coming back from the dead,' said Hazel. 'Yes, precisely.'

'I miss him already,' Hazel said. 'And Mrs Bagshaw.'

'Yes, I know,' said Nurse Griddle. 'I ask only this: please do not do what I have done and allow his disappearance to define you. You cannot live your life waiting for something to happen. You have to make it happen.'

'I want to become a chef.'

Nurse Griddle squeezed her hand even tighter. 'Then I know you shall. You are a capable girl, Hazel Bagshaw. You owe it to yourself to make the most of your life.'

Packing Up Books

It had been a month since the incident with Millicent Hartwell, and things had changed at Thornthwaite Manor. Old Tom and Nurse Griddle did nothing to dissuade the twins from selling. Uncle Harry stayed on to oversee the sale. While Hazel was recovering, the twins helped out with the household chores, and they continued to do so even once she was better.

Millicent and Felicia no longer visited. Adam had not returned either, but Lorelli had written to ask him about Millicent. When the reply came, she read the letter in private before sharing the relevant details with her brother. Millicent, it turned out, was a very good liar. Doctor Mingus thought she was making good progress but when Mrs Hartwell walked out on her husband and daughter, Millicent couldn't deal with the rejection. She retreated into a world in which the lines between reality and fantasy were increasingly blurred. No one knew where the Hartwells went following the incident, but the butcher's had been empty ever since.

The Cricks remained, although Felicia no longer spoke to Lorelli or Ovid. She avoided eye contact with them at school and on the bus home. Still, when Lorelli announced she was getting off at the stop at Little Fledgling, Ovid assumed it had something to do with Felicia.

'You haven't made up with her, have you?' he asked anxiously.

Felicia was sitting a couple of seats in front of them.

Lorelli lowered her voice. 'No, Felicia made it clear that we are no longer friends and I'm rather relieved about that.'

'Then where are you going?'

'To the library.'

'You mean to work on your novel?' asked Ovid.

Lorelli pressed the button to stop the bus. 'I didn't know you knew.'

Ovid smirked. 'You know our secrets never stay hidden for long.'

'I'm scared it won't be any good,' replied Lorelli.

'So what if it's not?' said Ovid. 'If it's no good, just write something else.'

The bus pulled up outside the sign that still read Hartwell's Rare Meat Emporium.

'Don't be late,' said Ovid. 'I'm cooking tonight. Hazel's teaching me one of Mrs Bagshaw's recipes. Six-nut nutloaf.'

'I can't wait,' replied Lorelli.

The bus doors opened and Felicia got off. Lorelli followed her off but kept her distance. She was expecting Felicia to ignore her as usual, so she was surprised when she turned around and asked, 'Is it true? Are you selling the manor?'

'Yes,' replied Lorelli.

'When are you leaving?'

'Uncle Harry says the sale should go through very soon.'

'Won't you be sorry to go?'

'Not at all.'

Lorelli said the words firmly but, if she was honest with herself, over the past few weeks her certainty about leaving the manor had ebbed away. When she told Uncle Harry of her doubts he said it was only natural to worry about making such a brave decision. Lorelli sensed that Ovid was having doubts too, but whenever she asked him he denied it.

'My parents say you're thinking of moving in there.' Felicia pointed to the empty butcher's shop.

'We might do,' said Lorelli. 'But I'm not sure Ovid is keen on that idea.'

Felicia's eyes misted over with sadness. 'Does he . . . ? Does he ask about me?'

Lorelli felt a rare moment of pity for Felicia. 'Yes. In fact, he was talking about you on the bus, just then.'

'I hope he isn't too upset about me breaking up with him,' said Felicia.

'He understands,' said Lorelli, hiding her smile.

'Goodnight then, Lori-chick— Lorelli. I'm sorry we're not friends any more.'

'I'm not sure we ever really were,' said Lorelli.

'No, you're probably right.'

Felicia left and Lorelli continued towards the library. On the walk over the bridge she noticed pink and white blossom on the trees. New buds had sprung up on the grassy verges of the road. For a moment she felt an unusual wave of optimism and hope about the future.

She pushed open the library door, eager to tell Miss Wilde her latest story idea. It was all about a World War One soldier trying to write a letter to his fiancée after learning that he was to be leading the attack into no man's land. She was ready to burst straight into it when she found Miss Wilde inside, packing books into boxes.

'What are you doing?' said Lorelli.

'I'm leaving,' said Miss Wilde.

'But why? Uncle Harry said he wouldn't shut the library.'

'And that was very kind of Uncle Harry,' said Miss Wilde. 'I very much hope he can honour his word, but you can't have a library without staff. I was a council employee. My job no longer exists.'

'But . . . but I can pay you . . .' began Lorelli.

Miss Wilde found a chair and sat. 'My dear Lorelli, as wonderful and generous as that is, I am beginning to feel like a charity case.'

'What's wrong with that?' said Lorelli. 'As long as we keep the library open, what does it matter?'

'It matters to me. A library shouldn't be a charitable institution that requires generous benefactors to subsidise it. It should be something everyone owns and everyone pays for. Libraries enrich our lives because they open up the world to those who most need it opened up.'

'Yes, I see that, but the council shut it down and we can keep it going. What else matters?' said Lorelli.

Miss Wilde threw another book into the box. 'Lorelli,' she said, 'I believe you will find a way to achieve everything you desire and I hope you do keep this library open, but my fate is not yours. You were right when you said I should take this as an opportunity. I'm leaving Little Fledgling.'

'But how will I write my story without you?'

'You don't need me,' said Miss Wilde. 'You don't need anyone. I told you, writing is like life; it is not something that can be taught. It is something you have to learn yourself. I believe this takes work and the ability to learn from your mistakes, but perhaps you are right and when you find your story it will flow out of you in one perfect stream. I doubt it, but that doesn't mean it isn't possible. I genuinely don't think anything is impossible for you.'

Killing the Past

After a surprisingly edible nutloaf that evening, the twins went to the games room. Lorelli had conceded the previous game, which meant it was Ovid's turn to be white. They set up the board and he was considering his first move when Uncle Harry stepped into the room and announced, 'Do you want the good news or the good news?'

'The good news,' said Ovid.

'I have found somewhere for Jenny to live. I'm in the process of acquiring a piece of land big enough that it will both satisfy the authorities, but also ensure her safety. Isn't that terrific?'

'That's great,' said Lorelli. 'What is the other good news?'

'This.' He placed a piece of paper on the chessboard. 'It's the completion document for the sale of the estate. It just requires your signatures.'

Ovid lifted it up to examine it. It was simply worded and included the large amount of money for the sale but made no mention of the buyer's name.

'And the buyer definitely won't build on the land?' said Lorelli.

'Don't worry about a thing,' replied Uncle Harry. 'It's all going to be exactly as I promised. So, what do you think? Are you ready to sign and move on with your lives?'

Ovid handed the document to Lorelli. He hadn't wanted to admit that the whole idea of selling left him rigid with fear. Thornthwaite Manor had been in their family for generations. The twins were the last surviving members of their bloodline. Selling felt like a betrayal of their ancestors. More than that, Thornthwaite Manor was his home.

Uncle Harry said, 'I don't want to rush you, but the way I look at it, if you're going to make a fresh start, why delay? Why wait?'

Lorelli picked up the pen. 'Yes,' she said. 'That's what I want. A fresh start.'

She signed it, then twisted it around and handed Ovid the pen. He looked at the document with his sister's name at the bottom. A few years ago, Lorelli had gone through a phase of practising her signature on any scrap of paper she could find. The end result was a carefully crafted piece of art with the L and the T towering over the lower case letters, creating two sides of a sloping roof that housed the rest of the name. Ovid scribbled his own name underneath.

'Well done,' said Uncle Harry. He picked up the piece of paper and folded it twice. He dropped it into his inside jacket pocket, from which he pulled out a second piece of paper. 'I also thought you might like to see this.

'What is it?' asked Ovid, leaning over to read it.

'It's an application for adoption.'

'Adoption?' repeated Lorelli.

'Yes, with your permission it would be my great honour to adopt you. I want to spend whatever time I have making things right. You're already in my will. Now, I would love for you to become Marshalls. The Thornthwaite name has plagued you too long.'

'Plagued?' repeated Ovid quietly.

Uncle Harry walked to the patio doors. The sun was low in the sky, giving the light a deep yellowish intensity. 'Martha fell in love with all this,' he said. 'The house, its history . . .'

'And our father,' added Lorelli.

'Yes, of course, your father. But none of it was real. People don't live like this any more. And yet the Thornthwaites have refused to let it go. That's what makes today such a momentous occasion. Finally, you've done what your forefathers were too afraid to do. You're saying goodbye to all this. I've been dreaming of this day since your parents' wedding.'

'The wedding where you got thrown out?' said Ovid.

'To my shame, yes, that's true. I may have overdone the wine and said some things that upset your mother.'

'What things?' asked Lorelli.

Uncle Harry took a deep breath and turned to face them. 'I told her I thought she was a fool to marry into this family. I told her I was scared for her life.'

'Why?'

'You've read the book. You know the history. Not one of your ancestors lived to a decent age. Not one.'

'What was the promise you made?' said Lorelli.

'I promised to look after you,' replied Uncle Harry, avoiding her gaze.

'At the wedding?' said Ovid. 'Before we were born? You promised to look after children who didn't even exist yet?'

Uncle Harry pushed open the doors. A light breeze moved the curtains.

'No more lies,' said Lorelli.

Uncle Harry stepped out onto the lawn. 'I told you, I was scared for my sister. Murder is like a genetic illness in this family. It is passed down from generation to generation. I was angry with her for her arrogance in thinking she could escape it. I was angry with your father for taking her away from me.'

'What did you promise?' Ovid followed him out.

An aeroplane shadow passed over Uncle Harry as he turned around and answered. 'I promised your father that if any harm came to Martha, I would tear down every brick of Thornthwaite Manor myself. I promised that if she died, the Thornthwaite line would die with her.'

'We're the Thornthwaite line,' said Lorelli, stepping over the threshold into the last of the evening's light.

'Yes, but if you allow me to adopt you, you needn't be,' said Uncle Harry.

'You want to kill our family?' said Ovid.

'Kill your family? No. I could never harm my sister's kids.'

'And what about tearing down every brick of Thornthwaite Manor?' asked Lorelli.

'You've sold it. What do you care what happens to it?' asked Uncle Harry.

'We sold it on the basis that the estate would go unspoilt,' said Lorelli.

'So it will. I promise, nothing will be built. Well, maybe a shelter for Jenny.'

'For Jenny?' said Ovid.

'*You're* the buyer,' said Lorelli.

'Yes,' said Uncle Harry. 'Don't worry, I paid the going rate. This isn't about money. This was never about money. This is about fulfilling my promise.'

Uncle Harry slowly reached into his pocket. In the dusky low light it was difficult to tell what he was taking out. Both twins imagined a gun, but it was not a gun. It was a small black box with a stubby aerial in the top.

'It's time to move on,' said Uncle Harry.

'What is that?' asked Ovid.

'It's a detonator. I'm bringing it down,' announced Uncle Harry. 'This is the only way to set you free.'

No Loose Ends

The Thornthwaite twins had never felt a telepathic connection, but as they listened to their uncle explain why he was going to blow up their house, Lorelli knew exactly what Ovid was thinking. Uncle Harry was crazy. He was willing to blow up Thornthwaite Manor to honour a promise made to someone who had died a long time ago.

'Where are the explosives?' asked Ovid.

'I placed them at the bottom of the southwest tower,' replied Uncle Harry. 'It's a structural key point. My experts tell me that when it comes down, it will bring the rest of the building with it. I'm not convinced, but if it doesn't, we have more explosives.'

'You can't blow up our house,' said Lorelli.

'It's my house now, and of course I can,' said Uncle Harry.

'Give us back the document,' said Lorelli.

'Yes. We no longer want to sell,' said Ovid.

Lorelli stepped forward, but Uncle Harry held the detonator out and placed his thumb on the large red button. 'I'm sorry, I can't do that,' he said. 'This is for your own good. All of this is for your own good.'

'You tricked us for our own good?' said Ovid.

'How did I trick you? It was your idea to sell,' protested Uncle Harry. 'What does it matter what happens to it now?'

'You've been manipulating us since you arrived,' said Lorelli.

Uncle Harry laughed in disbelief. 'What have I manipulated?'

'Since gaining our confidence you have been turning us against this place, making us feel as though the manor was responsible for the horror of our family history.'

'Now, Lorelli . . .' Uncle Harry protested.

'That's right,' Ovid interrupted. 'You made us think of our home as evil, but it's just a building.'

'No, it's not,' he snapped. 'Thornthwaite Manor is the villain. Murder and death are built into the walls of this place,' said Uncle Harry. 'You didn't need me to tell you that.'

'You've lied to us and deceived us since the start,' said Lorelli. 'Is the weak heart even true?'

'Of course it is,' said Uncle Harry. 'That's the whole point. My time is limited. I have no future. But you do. That's why I have put you in my will. The only way to make your future bright is to extinguish the past.'

'The servants are all in there,' said Lorelli.

'Don't worry, I've worked the whole thing out. It will look like an accident. I'll explain that I demolished my own property, as I have a right to do, but that I was unaware your servants had refused to leave. We'll tell the authorities that we thought the house was clear for demolition. It's not like there are any other witnesses. It's just us.'

'Put the detonator down,' said Lorelli. 'We'll agree to anything you want if you let the others live.'

'I'm afraid I can't do that, and don't think about warning them either,' said Uncle Harry. 'If you take one step inside that house, I swear I'll bring it down.'

'On us?' said Ovid.

'I'm not worried about you. You two are born survivors. You'll get out when you need to.'

'But why? Why would you want to kill them?'

'It needs to be clean. No loose ends.'

'They aren't loose ends,' said Lorelli. 'They're people.'

'Yes, but one uncle is enough. Now, I'm tired of this. It's time.'

Uncle Harry pressed the button.

The explosion was instant. The ground shook and flocks of birds took to the air. A flash of light filled the sky, followed by clouds of black smoke.

'We have to get the others out!' Lorelli turned to run into the house but Ovid held her back. 'What are you doing?' she fought him off. 'Everyone is in there –'

'Look at the smoke,' he said.

Lorelli looked again and understood what he meant. It wasn't coming from the building. The southwest tower stood untouched. The twins turned to Uncle Harry, but he looked just as confused.

'It's coming from something around the side,' said Lorelli.

'What's on that side of the manor?' asked Ovid.

Uncle Harry turned white. 'My car.'

All three of them ran around the side of the house, where they saw the source of the smoke. Uncle Harry's car was on fire. The roof had been torn to shreds. There were car parts strewn all over the grass. The windscreen had shattered and there was a strong smell of burning rubber. One of the doors had flown off and landed on a rose bush.

'My car . . . my beautiful car . . . How? How has this happened?'

Dragos, Tom, Nurse Griddle and Hazel appeared out of a side door and gathered to watch. Tom and Dragos both carried fire extinguishers.

Uncle Harry turned to face them. 'What have you done?' he snarled.

'I find explosives at base of southwest tower,' said Dragos. 'This is very dangerous. That is why I put them somewhere safe.'

'Safe?' said Nurse Griddle. 'I'm not sure this counts as safe.' She motioned towards the burning car.

'It's my roses I'm worried about,' said Old Tom.

'Roses?' cried Uncle Harry. 'Who cares about roses? That car was a classic. It's irreplaceable.'

'Only people are irreplaceable,' said Lorelli.

Dragos approached. 'Please, into the house,' he said. 'We must make this safe.'

'You,' growled Uncle Harry.

'Yes, me.'

'You did this.' Uncle Harry squared up to him. 'Do you have any idea how much that car was worth?'

'No, I have no interest in cars. Please step aside,' said Dragos.

'No!' yelled Uncle Harry. 'I own this manor. I own this estate. All of you are trespassing!'

'Safety comes first,' said Dragos. 'I will put out fire first. It could spread. Please step aside.'

'I will not.' Uncle Harry blocked his way.

'Very well.' Dragos aimed the nozzle at Uncle Harry and squeezed the trigger. A jet of white foam flew out and knocked Uncle Harry spluttering and tumbling to the ground.

'Good shot, Dragos,' said Ovid.

'You oafish barbarian!' cried Uncle Harry. 'I'll have my lawyers on you.' Bits of foam flew from his mouth as he shouted, but Dragos wasn't listening. He and Tom were busily trying to get the fire under control.

'Get off my property!' shouted Uncle Harry.

The twins stepped up close to him.

'It's not your property.' Lorelli plucked the document out of Uncle Harry's pocket. He tried to stop her but Ovid held his wrists.

'It's ours,' added Ovid.

Lorelli tore the document in half, then handed both pieces of paper to Ovid. He tore it again and passed it back. It went back and forth several times until all that was left were bits of paper, which they scattered over Uncle Harry.

He stood up and pushed them out of his way. 'You ungrateful little . . . I only wanted to help you,' he said. 'I only wanted to put things right.'

'By destroying our home and murdering our servants?' said Ovid.

'By removing our family name from history?' said Lorelli.

Uncle Harry wiped the foam from his face. 'Yes, but I only did it for you. You're still my sister's kids.'

'Our mother was a Marshall,' said Ovid, 'but our father was a Thornthwaite.'

'And so are we,' said Lorelli.

'You've made that patently clear,' snarled Uncle Harry. 'I tried to save you from yourselves, but you two are beyond saving. There's something wrong with you. You're not normal.'

'I think I can live with that,' said Lorelli.

'Yes, me too,' added Ovid.

Good Riddance
to Bad Uncle

By the time Tom and Dragos had put out the fire Uncle Harry had gone. The twins had heard him call a taxi as he walked away. When the taxi-coordinator asked where he was going he replied, 'Anywhere but here. Just make it quick. I'll pay double, triple. Just get me away from this place.'

With the fire extinguished, the others could all see the extent of the damage. The elegant piece of classic engineering was barely recognisble as a car.

'At the risk of sounding like Mrs Bagshaw, I think we all need a strong cup of tea after all this excitement,' said Nurse Griddle. 'Shall we, Hazel?'

'Yes, mother. I made some biscuits this morning.'

'One of Mrs Bagshaw's recipes?'

'No. One of my own.'

Hazel and Nurse Griddle went in, while the twins remained with Dragos and Old Tom by the car.

'This is good riddance to bad uncle,' said Dragos.

'He said something about one uncle being enough,' said Lorelli. 'What did he mean?'

'Don't ask us,' said Old Tom quickly.

Dragos placed a hand on his shoulder. 'Tom, no more lies.' he said. 'They deserve honesty now. They should know.'

'Know what?' asked the twins.

Tom pulled out his pair of old secateurs. 'Did I ever tell you about these old clippers?'

'Enough about plants,' interrupted Lorelli. 'Just tell us what he meant.'

'Your uncle knew the truth about me,' said Dragos.

'About your father?' said Ovid.

'About my mother.'

'What?' said the twins in unison.

'My father was a prospector who never found gold,' said Dragos. 'My mother was better gold digger. She was different kind of gold digger. Her name was Alexandreira. She was beautiful and greedy. She hoped my father would make her rich with all his talk of gold. But talk is all it was. When he did not live up to expectations she turned to your grandfather. As I said, she was beautiful and ambitious. The only thing that stood in her way was his wife.'

'You're talking about Silas's first wife, Mabel?' said Ovid. 'The one who died in the gas explosion down the mine?'

'Yes,' said Dragos. 'My mother tricked my father and Lady Mabel Thornthwaite into going down that mine. My mother made the explosion.'

'She murdered Lady Thornthwaite and your father?' said Lorelli, struggling to keep up.

'She killed her ladyship, yes, but my father escaped. Except he now knew his wife was trying to kill him. He took their

270

son . . .' Dragos removed his hat and wiped his brow with the back of his hand, leaving a black sooty mark across his face. 'He took me to Romania. With him and Lady Thornthwaite gone, my mother was free to marry Lord Thornthwaite.'

'So your mother was our grandmother,' asked Lorelli.

'Yes.'

'Meaning you're our uncle?' said Ovid.

'Half-uncle,' said Dragos. 'If there is such a thing.'

'Is that why you came back?' asked Ovid. 'To claim your part of the inheritance?'

'If I was going to do this I would already have done so. No. That is not why I am here. I have no interest in your money. I came to help preserve this magnificent building you call home. I came to save the old lady.'

'So Uncle Harry was talking about you?' said Lorelli.

'Not just about me.' Dragos looked at Tom.

'So these old clippers . . .' he began.

'Tom!' said Lorelli. 'Just tell us the truth.'

Tom nodded, then spoke slowly. 'I don't want this to make any difference to how you treat me. It's all just stuff and history.'

'What is?' said Lorelli.

'Silas had already had a child with his first wife, Lady Mabel,' said Tom, 'but Lady Agnes wanted her son to be the one who inherited. If she'd had her way, she'd have had your father adopted or . . . worse. As luck would have it, Silas was not totally without sentiment. Both boys were his sons, after all. Still, he wanted to please his new wife, so he compromised. He had the lad's name changed, then had him adopted by one of the servants and kept on at the manor.'

271

'And the son's name?' Ovid already knew the answer.

'Thomas Paine, young master.'

'So you're our uncle too?' said Lorelli.

'Half-uncle, like Dragos,' said Old Tom. 'Your grandfather was my old man.'

'Then the estate belongs to you as much as it belongs to us,' said Ovid.

Tom smiled and gazed out across the lawn towards Avernus Lake and beyond. 'What you've never really understood is that the estate don't much care who owns it. You try telling one of them great oaks you've got in Huxley Woods that it's yours. You try telling Avernus Lake that you're in charge. No, this estate don't belong to anyone. The way I see it, I grew up here the same as my roses.'

'But why did you never tell us?' said Lorelli.

'Because you'd have treated me differently, and I like things as they are. So I take it you're no longer leaving the old place.'

There was no need to confer. 'We're staying. We won't sell,' said Lorelli.

'Never,' said Ovid.

'Good. Now, these old clippers,' said Tom, 'they were given to me by my old man as a birthday present. The only present he ever gave me, unless you count that row of trees he had planted down on the main road the day I was born.' Tom snipped the secateurs together and grinned.

'You never got another birthday present?' said Ovid.

'Not one,' said Tom. 'I asked him why once. D'you know what he said? He told me that he had already given me everything he had to give. What do you make of that?'

'It was his way of giving you the estate?' said Ovid.

'No,' said Lorelli, 'it meant that the estate would provide you with food and shelter, but that the secateurs would help you tend to its needs. It's a metaphor.'

'No. This is not it,' said Dragos. 'He was giving you job. He was saying, son, go be a gardener.'

'Could be any of those things,' said Old Tom. 'Or none of them. Most likely it was just Silas being mean. But he's gone now, the trees are still there and these clippers still work like they're brand new.' He snipped off two white roses, both badly burnt by the fire, and handed one to Lorelli and the other to Ovid.

'I'm sorry about your roses,' said Lorelli.

'There's no need to worry,' said Old Tom. 'The roses may be done for, but the roots are still strong and that's the most important thing.' He placed a hand on each of the twins' shoulders and gave them a gentle squeeze. 'Good day, young masters.'

'Good day, Tom,' replied Lorelli and Ovid.

A New Story

The previous year, the great fire had reduced much of the twins' home to a shell. So many rooms had been laid to waste. So many priceless artefacts had gone up in smoke. Irreplaceable pictures were turned to ash. But as is the way with shells, life had emerged from within the crisp remains.

When Lorelli thought back on why she had decided to leave Thornthwaite Manor, she was unsure how much she could pin on Uncle Harry. He had certainly done his best to influence her, always describing it in terms of a prison, a cage or a death trap. He had talked about the possibilities of escape and making a fresh start. He had instructed Beaufort to make a meal that left them with a feeling of unease about the house, but, in the end, it had been Lorelli's own decision.

The reasons for wanting to leave may have been murky, but she knew the exact moment she had decided to stay. It was Uncle Harry's speech about making things right by destroying a building. If life at Thornthwaite Manor had taught her anything, it was that destruction could not be combatted with more destruction. The only way to progress was to acknowledge what had come before, no matter how terrible it was, then choose a different path.

Lorelli realised she was overthinking it. She thought so much her head hurt. She didn't know what to do with all her overflowing thoughts, so she sat down at her desk and wrote. This time there was no need to research any background or create any characters. She didn't worry about the story arc or the style. She didn't have a plan. She didn't even have a premise. She simply wrote everything in her head, until it began to take form on the page and then she found her beginning. She realised she was writing a book about an old manor house full of secrets and stories. There were people too, but it was the house that was the central character. Lorelli liked the story. It felt different. It felt real. She hoped she would reach the end of it this time.

The Thornthwaite Family
1737 to Present

Lord Oliver Thornthwaite = Lady Mary Thornthwaite
1737 ~ 1790   1751 ~ 1790

Lord Allegro Thornthwaite = Lady Enoch Thornthwaite
1787 ~ 1824   1788 ~ 1839

Lord Millard Thornthwaite = Lady Edwina Thornthwaite
1808 ~ 1838   1805 ~ 1837

Lord Bristol Thornthwaite = Lady Asia Thornthwaite
1832 ~ 1867   1832 ~ 1867

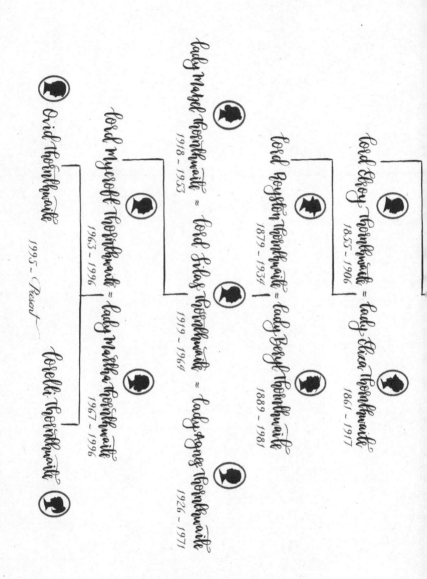

Lord Elroy Thornthwaite = Lady Eliza Thornthwaite
1855 ~ 1906   1861 ~ 1917

Lady Mabel Thornthwaite = Lord Peyston Thornthwaite = Lady Beryl Thornthwaite
1918 ~ 1953   1879 ~ 1934   1889 ~ 1981

Lord Myecroft Thornthwaite = Lord Silas Thornthwaite = Lady Agnes Thornthwaite
1963 ~ 1996   1919 ~ 1964   1926 ~ 1971

Lord Myecroft Thornthwaite = Lady Matha Thornthwaite
1963 ~ 1996   1967 ~ 1996

Orid Thornthwaite   Loselli Thornthwaite
1995 ~ Present

The Thornthwaite Legacy

The Thornthwaite Inheritance was published by Bloomsbury in July 2009, which means that at some point in 2008 I pitched a six-word book idea to my publisher, Sarah.

'Twins trying to kill each other,' I said.

'Yes, write that,' she replied.

Since publication, *The Thornthwaite Inheritance* has visited many countries, made lots of friends and collected seven awards.

So why has it taken me so long to write the sequel?

The answer is called Lotta.

She has been my Swedish editor since she first bought the rights to the book, but I only met her in 2015 when I was invited to the Litteralund festival. During our day together she repeatedly asked me if I would write another Thornthwaite book. Eventually – to stop her going on – I found an outline of a sequel called *The Thornthwaite Betrayal*, written back in 2012. She read it very quickly then said, 'Yes, write this.'

Thank you, Lotta. I hope you like this book.

I am also indebted to everyone at Piccadilly Press, including my fabulous editors, Georgia and Talya. The design team did a great job with the cover and I was over the moon that Adam Stower agreed to do the artwork again. Thank you to my friends at Bloomsbury for continuing to support the first book. My wife, Lisa, was, as usual, invaluable as my harshest (but fairest) critic. Sylvie and Bruce Marks provided inspiration for the glassblowing-related deaths. My Twitter friends gave support, distraction and ideas. Thanks to all the wonderful teachers who share my books with their students (a special thanks to Jon Biddle for encouraging his students to make a trailer for the first book). And finally, thank you to every reader who has bought and enjoyed my books. I have the best job in the world and am deeply grateful to everyone who makes that possible.

Gareth P. Jones

Gareth is the annoying younger brother of Adam. Adam has never tried to kill Gareth, although the thought must have crossed his mind once or twice.

These days, Gareth also spends his time annoying his wife, Lisa and their two children, Herbie and Autumn. As well as being annoying, Gareth sometimes writes books for children of all ages, visits schools, performs at music festivals and produces television. If you want to experience how annoying he can be, visit his website www.garethwrites.co.uk or follow him on Twitter: @jonesgarethp

Piccadilly
P R E S S

Thank you for choosing a Piccadilly Press book.

If you would like to know more about our authors, our books or if you'd just like to know what we're up to, you can find us online.

www.piccadillypress.co.uk

You can also find us on:

We hope to see you soon!